X

I want
to be an
Angel

Also by Jamila Gavin

Three Indian Princesses
The Magic Orange Tree
Kamla and Kate
Kamla and Kate Again
Ali and the Robot
The Hideaway
The Singing Bowls

I want to be an Angel

Stories by
JAMILA GAVIN

MAMMOTH

First published in Great Britain 1990
by Methuen Children's Books Ltd
Published 1991 by Mammoth
an imprint of Mandarin Paperbacks
Michelin House, 81 Fulham Road, London SW3 6RB

Mandarin is an imprint of the Octopus Publishing Group,
a division of Reed International Books Ltd

ISBN 0 7497 0987 1

A CIP catalogue record for this title
is available from the British Library

Printed in Great Britain
by Cox & Wyman Ltd, Reading, Berkshire

Contents

1
I Want to be an Angel

Her name was Epiphany Victoria Johnson, but everyone called her 'Effie'.

'She's God's own child,' her mother often enthused and no one liked to contradict her. Where would the family be without little Effie?

Effie was called 'little' Effie because she was quite short for her age. She was ten years old, but no one who knew her let that deceive them. She was as strong as an ox, and just as well, as every day she had to support the huge body of her invalid mother and help her from bed to wheelchair to bathroom to wheelchair, and finally, at the end of the day, back to bed again.

Even the nights weren't her own. Mrs Johnson couldn't roll over in bed by herself, and Effie had never forgotten the sight of those terrible bedsores her mother got because she hadn't been able to move. So, ever since Mr Johnson got fed up and disappeared into thin air, it was Effie who three times a night heard her mother call, 'Effie, darling, come and turn me over!' And Effie would slip out of bed, roll her mother over, go back to bed and fall fast asleep again.

Having a mother to take care of was hard enough, but Effie also had to see to her brother, Jackson and sister, Seraphina.

Jackson was eight and a right tearaway. Seraphina was only five and still like a baby. Luckily, they all went to the same school, but every morning Effie had to get them up, dressed, give them their breakfast and get them to school on time.

By the time Effie got to school, she had already been working about two hours. No wonder she sometimes fell asleep over her desk.

One day, the lady from the Social Services came round for a chat. She had heard about the family's difficulties and wanted to help. When she learned that Mr Johnson had gone away and was never coming back, she suggested that it might be sensible to put the children into care. She said that Mrs Johnson could move to a special flat designed for invalids and the children found good foster homes.

Great tears rolled down Mrs Johnson's cheeks and she asked: 'Would the children stay together?'

The lady looked vague. 'Of course we would

do our best. The girls would certainly stay together, but it may be difficult to have the boy as well . . .'

This was too much for Effie. She had been listening in quiet horror, her mouth opening wider and wider as if a huge scream was forcing open her throat. She came hurtling across the room and stood like a warrior next to her mother's wheelchair.

'No, no, no!' The words finally tumbled out. 'Me and Jackson and Seraphina, we're not going nowhere, do you hear? You can't take us away from our mum. You can't just go giving us to other families like we were sweets. We're managing just fine; O.K. hunky-dory, aren't we, Mum?'

Mrs Johnson sobbed even louder. Jackson and Seraphina came running when they heard the commotion, and when Seraphina saw her mother crying, she began hollering too.

'Now look what you've gone and done,' raged little Effie. 'Go away!'

'Effie, darling,' Mrs Johnson struggled to control herself. 'Effie, darling, the lady's only trying to help. You mustn't be rude.'

'We can take care of ourselves. I can do everything Mum can do. This is our home and this is where we'll stay.' As Effie finished her speech. Her voice had become quieter and quieter as if she knew she would have more chance of success by sounding grown-up.

The lady responded with an understanding smile. 'You've done a wonderful job, dear, and as your mother says, I'm only here to help you. Of course I don't want to split you up, but you do have far too much work for a little girl of your age. I don't suppose you get much time to play, do you?'

Effie was silent. No she didn't. She could hardly remember the last time she had gone down to the swings with her friends.

'Is there anyone, a relative perhaps, who could come and housekeep for you, or call in regularly?'

The Johnsons looked blankly at her. 'I'll leave you to discuss it among yourselves and come back in a week or two to see how you are getting on.'

When the lady had gone, the children clustered round their mother. Seraphina stopped crying and clambered on to her mother's lap. Leaning her head back on her mother's comforting bosom, she put her thumb in her mouth and looked at Effie with large pleading eyes.

Jackson stood at his mother's side and fiddled with the fringe of her blanket. He looked at Effie as if to say, 'Well? Are you going to sort this out?'

Effie looked at all three of them. 'We'll find someone,' she said defiantly.

Effie thought about it all day and all night.

Who could, who would come and look after them? She thought about it in school, and didn't stop even when Mrs Freeman said that rehearsals for the Christmas nativity play were about to begin.

'I shall hold auditions for the main parts,' she told the children. 'If anyone wants to learn a poem or read something for me, then come here next Friday lunchtime.'

For the first time since she had been at Cabot Junior School Effie didn't show any interest. Even though Effie's dearest and most secret wish, a secret she hadn't told anyone, was to be an angel. She had always wanted to be an angel. She could cry when she thought how much she wanted to put on a long, white, flowing dress, to have a silver band with a halo strapped to her head and a pair of silver cardboard wings fixed to her shoulder blades.

Every Christmas, when the teacher was choosing people for the nativity play, Effie had sat with clenched fists and her eyes tightly closed in prayer, 'Please, God let me be an angel.' But though she had once been a shepherd and once the innkeeper's wife, she had never been an angel.

Now she was in her last year at junior school. Next year she would be at the local comprehensive and she knew they didn't do things like that. It was her last chance to be an angel.

But Effie showed no interest. All she could think of was who could look after them so that they wouldn't have to go into care.

'I'll find somebody,' she whispered fiercely. 'I've got to.'

She made a list of all the grown-ups who could come and look after them. She listed them in order of those she liked best. Top of the list was Yuteford Johnson, her grown-up cousin.

Yuteford would be easy to ask because he lived in a house which they passed every day on their way to and from school. So the next day, after school, Effie told Jackson and Seraphina that they would call in on Yuteford and ask him to come and look after them.

Their eyes shone with excitement at the idea. As usual, Jackson got carried away and began to behave stupidly. As they walked along towards Nelson Road where Yuteford lived, he kept leaping up and down on to people's garden walls and dodging in and out of gateways. When they arrived at the house, Jackson flew down the path yelling at the top of his voice, 'Yuteford! Hey, Yuteford!'

An upstairs sash window flew up with an accusing crash. Mrs Elijah, the landlady, with her hair all in twists and curlers leaned out like an opera singer.

'Epiphany Johnson! Just what do you think

you're doing wandering about the streets with your brother and sister causing a nuisance? Does your mother know where you are?'

'I'm looking for Yuteford,' said Effie stoutly, not being put off. She knew Mrs Elijah was always poking her nose into other people's business – especially Yuteford's.

'He's asleep. You should know that.' Mrs Elijah wagged her finger. 'He works all night and sleeps all day, so you'd better get on home and stop disturbing everyone.'

Of course Effie knew that Yuteford worked all night and slept all day. He was lead guitarist with the Down Town Rats Rock Band, but it was after four o'clock, and Effie thought he might be waking up now.

Jackson was being cheeky. He pulled faces at Mrs Elijah and jumped over her flower beds, chanting, 'Yuteford, Yuteford!'

'It's time something was done about taking you children in hand,' Mrs Elijah exploded indignantly.

The front door opened with a fumble. Instinctively, the children retreated down the path. A head of tangled dreadlocks peered round the door. It was Yuteford. Effie sighed with relief as she saw him blinking like a sleepy old owl at the unfamiliar daylight.

'Did I hear my name?' Yuteford drawled in his deep, smoky-thick voice.

Seraphina and Jackson hurtled towards him and threw themselves on top of him.

'I hope we didn't wake you,' murmured Effie apologetically trying to disentangle the children from round his neck. 'I just wanted to ask you something.'

'Of course, of course, precious! Come on in.' He bowed low in the doorway and swept them through with a whisk of his hand. The upstairs window slammed shut.

Yuteford's room was still in darkness. The curtains were drawn tightly shut and the air was hung with the smell of beer and cigarettes.

Effie screwed up her nose. Seraphina came and took her hand clingingly, but Jackson, unperturbed, went roaming round the room looking for things to touch and fiddle with. Yuteford hurled some magazines off the sofa and ashtrays from the arms of the chairs.

'Sit down, sit down,' he entreated good-naturedly. 'It's been a while since I saw my little cousins.'

'I . . . er . . .' Effie faltered. Suddenly her proposal seemed absurd. Yuteford could hardly look after himself let alone come and look after them. 'I . . . er . . . wondered if you knew of anyone who could come and look after us all. The lady came from the Social Services, and she says if no one comes to help, me, Jackson and Seraphina will have to go into care . . .and . . .' she tailed away miserably.

14

'Gee, man!' Yuteford exclaimed sympathetically. 'They can't do that!'

'You come, Yuteford!' cried Jackson.

'Yeh, you come, Yuteford,' echoed Seraphina.

Effie frowned at them, her eyes trying to signal 'no'. 'Yuteford couldn't possibly,' she said. 'He doesn't keep the same hours, and besides, Mum couldn't put up with the drinking and smoking.'

'But, Effie,' wailed Jackson in outraged protest. 'You said . . .

'Yes, Effie, you said . . .' chorused Seraphina.

'Do you know anyone, Yuteford?' asked Effie hastily.

'We want you, Yuteford! Don't we, Seraphina,' insisted Jackson.

'Yeh, yeh, yeh!' laughed Yuteford, tossing himself into the easy chair. 'You want me to come and housekeep for you? Be your nanny or something? Gee, kids, you must be bonkers!' Then he stopped laughing, and with a big sigh, closed his eyes. 'Oh man!' he whispered. 'That's what I call a predicament.'

'What's a predicasent?' asked Seraphina.

'Ssssh!' silenced Effie. She could see that Yuteford was thinking. It made her feel better. It was good to have someone think for her.

'Aunt Bernice!' Yuteford suggested as he swung himself into a sitting position. 'No?' He took in the lack of enthusiasm on their faces.

'She's too holy,' said Effie.

'She makes us pray all the time,' added Jackson.

'What's a predicasent?' repeated Seraphina insistently. She was ignored.

'Yeh! S'pose you're right,' sighed Yuteford, subsiding back into the chair. 'Uncle Don and Aunt Corinne?' He opened one eye questioningly.

Effie shook her head. 'Uncle Don hates children and Aunt Corinne suffers from dizzy spells.'

Jackson was bored and went wandering over to the guitar propped in the window.

'How about Cousin Esmé? Now she's a motherly sort of person, isn't she?' continued Yuteford.

Effie shrugged her shoulders. She felt embarrassed. Yuteford was trying so hard to be helpful, but none of his suggestions was any good.

'Well . . .' She raised her eyebrows as if it were a possibility worth considering, though inside she was shrieking no, no, no, definitely NOT Cousin Esmé. She always smelt of lavender talcum powder, and Effie couldn't stand the smell of lavender. 'Well . . .' she said again. Crash! 'Jackson!' Effie screamed with dismay. He had dropped the guitar.

Yuteford shouted words which Mrs Johnson

would not have approved of in front of children, but he was really angry. Jackson flew over to Effie. 'Sorry, Yuteford,' he blabbered.

'You blithering idiot!' stormed Yuteford tenderly retrieving his precious instrument. 'You're nothing but a vandal!'

Effie clasped the hands of her brother and sister and backed towards the door. 'Sorry, Yuteford,' she stammered. 'Hope it isn't broken.'

There was a long pause while he examined it, then to their relief, he turned round beaming all over. 'I should tan your hide!' He pounced on Jackson and turned him upside down. 'You won't get anyone wanting to take you on!' he joked.

The children said goodbye and Yuteford promised to go on thinking about it. As they walked solemnly home, Effie gave a deep, deep sigh. She knew the problem was always going to be Jackson. Who would manage him?

'Effie,' murmured Seraphina gently, looking up at her big sister. 'What's a predicasent?'

'Predicament,' corrected Effie. 'I think it means a problem.'

Somehow it had been easier to manage while it was still summer. Easier to get up in the morning, easier to walk to school, easier for Effie to nip home at lunch time to see her mother, and easier on summer evenings, when the children could play out in front most of the time where she could see them from the window. There was a safe feeling about summer.

But once October came and they put the clocks back, Effie found it much harder going. She hated getting up and dressing while it was still dark outside; she hated setting off for school in the misty gloom of orange sodium street lamps, and the menacing sweep of car headlights; and arguing with Jackson to keep on his anorak, and running back along damp pavements to look for a glove which Seraphina had dropped. There just seemed so many more things to think about.

Only when the first signs of Christmas began to appear in the shops did Effie begin to feel a thrill of excitement. She often overheard the mothers grumbling. 'Christmas seems to start earlier and earlier every year,' they moaned. But for Effie, it couldn't start early enough. It gave her something to look forward to. She loved the shop windows bursting with gifts for Christmas; she loved the brightness, the colour, the music, the putting up of Christmas decorations, the singing of carols, the making of Christmas cards, and most of all, she loved the school nativity play.

The day of the auditions suddenly arrived. At school that Friday morning there was an excited murmuring of practised lines and high expectations. After lunch, a cluster of children, some with poetry books in hand, gathered in Mrs Freeman's classroom. Effie was still out in the playground when Mrs Freeman passed by.

'Aren't you coming, Effie?' she asked with surprise. Effie was usually the first to try to get a part in the school nativity play.

'Come along, come along,' she urged, not waiting for an answer.

As her teacher strode on ahead, Effie thought, 'I suppose I can still remember the lines the angel said to the shepherds.' She began to whisper them as she made her way across the playground . . .' Born this night in the city of David is a baby who will be Christ the King. They will call his name, Jesus, and you will find him in a stable marked by a star . . .'

'Effie, Effie!' one of her friends called her urgently. 'Your brother's gone and thrown Matthew Kilroy's trainers on to the terrapin roof!'

Effie halted in dismay. Then she tried to ignore the information and began walking again towards Mrs Freeman's classroom.

'Effie! Are you deaf or something? Jackson's gone and thrown Matthew Kilroy's trainers on the terrapin roof. His mum won't half be mad. They're brand new and cost a packet.'

'Where's Jackson?' she asked wearily.

'I dunno. Run off somewhere,' replied her friend.

Effie changed direction. She broke into a run. She would have to sort it out before going to the audition. Last time Jackson threw someone's welly boot over the fence and into the canal, Mrs Johnson had had to buy a new pair, and she really couldn't afford it. Trainers would be worse. Oh dear, there would be such trouble.

Lots of children came running towards her. 'Effie, Effie, Jackson's been a naughty boy!'

'Where is he?' bellowed Effie, sounding mad.

'Hiding,' said a voice smugly.

Effie looked up at the terrapin roof in despair. How could she possibly get up there? Even if she stood on Darrel Evan's back – and he was the tallest boy in the school – she would never be able to climb up on to the roof.

'My mum won't half be mad,' stated Matthew Kilroy, solemnly studying the holes in his socks. 'You'll have to buy me some new ones.'

'I'm going to get them back,' muttered Effie. She looked at the drainpipe. She took off her shoes and socks.

'Watcha gonna do, Effie?' asked a voice.

'Get the trainers,' replied Effie simply. After all, she was considered quite a good climber. She could shin up the ropes in the gym better than anybody. She took hold of the drainpipe with both hands, and lifted one foot on to the first wall fitting.

A ripple of admiration spread through the crowd of children. 'Effie's climbing the drainpipe!'

Effie gave a little jerk and got both feet on to the wall of the terrapin. She was stuck. She didn't know how to shuffle her hands upwards. She wriggled her bottom, but that didn't get her anywhere. The children broke out chanting. 'Go on, Effie! Effie, Effie, Effie!'

'Epiphany Johnson, just what do you think you are up to?' A stern voice scattered the crowd. Effie felt two firm hands grip her round the waist and lift her down. Mrs Cottle, the teacher on dinner duty, then stood back and surveyed her with shocked displeasure. 'I think you had better go and see the head immediately.'

'But . . .' Effie exclaimed desperately. 'But,' she had wanted to cry, 'I've got to get the trainers back and then I've got to get to the auditions. I do so want to be an angel.' But her words never got out of her mouth. Mrs Cottle simply pointed towards the Head's office and said, 'Make your excuses to Miss Redford.'

Some days are like that, just plain bad. Nothing seems to go right. But Effie felt that this Friday was one of the worst in living memory. The Head, Miss Redford, had told her that she and Jackson had let everybody down, especially her mother; she had missed

21

the audition, and worst of all, she couldn't think of anyone who would come and look after them.

After school, as they walked home, Effie was silent, Jackson surly and in a kicking mood. Seraphina was over the moon because she had been given a part in the nativity play. She hopscotched ahead of her brother and sister chanting, 'I'm in the play! I'm in the play! I'm gonna be a lamb! I'm gonna be a lamb!'

'Who's going to be Mary, then?' asked Effie, miserably.

'Zoë Calloway,' answered Seraphina knowledgeably. 'They chose Zoë.'

'They would,' muttered Effie ungraciously. She had decided that teachers always chose girls like Zoë to play Mary in nativity plays; girls who had long, straight, blonde hair, with pale thin faces and blue eyes, and who looked holy.

'Ben Potter is Joseph and Jonathan Aldridge is Herod. I like Jonathan,' sighed Seraphina.

'Who's playing Angel Gabriel?' Effie almost choked over the question.

'Carlene,' beamed Seraphina. 'I think she'll look lovely, don't you, Effie?'

'Hmmm,' grunted Effie shortly. Carlene was her friend so she couldn't begrudge her the part.

When they got home, Mrs Johnson saw immediately that all was not well.

'What's up, little Effie?' she asked sympathetically. 'What's up, Jackson?'

'Jackson's been a naughty boy,' announced Seraphina, climbing up on to her mother's lap. 'He threw Matthew Kilroy's trainers up on to the terrapin roof. Matthew says we'll have to pay.'

'Oh, Jackson!' exclaimed Mrs Johnson with dismay.

'We were all throwing things,' grunted Jackson, kicking the settee.

'Effie tried to climb the drainpipe to get them back . . . and Effie got sent to Miss Redford . . . and Effie didn't come to the auditions, so she didn't get a part in the nativity . . . but I did, Mum, I'm going to be a lamb!' Seraphina finished her speech with a triumphant flourish.'

'But what about the trainers?' asked Mrs Johnson, still agitated at the thought of having to pay for a new pair.

'It's O.K., Mum, the caretaker got them down,' Effie reassured her.

There was a knock on the door. It was Yuteford. Hanging on to his arm, as if afraid she might topple off her stiletto high heels, was a very glamorous young woman in a tight slinky dress.

'Hi, Effie! Is it O.K. to call?' He peered past Effie who had opened the door and waved at Mrs Johnson. 'Hi, Aunty! It's me, Yuteford!

23

I've brought a friend along. We've got a proposition for you.'

'Come right in, Yuteford!' cried Mrs Johnson warmly.

Yuteford took the woman's elbow and urged her forward. 'Aunty, I'd like you to meet Loretta.'

As Yuteford made the introductions, Effie studied Loretta critically. She was very beautiful.

'Are you a pop star?' asked Jackson.

'I think she's a witch,' said Seraphina warily eyeing Loretta's exceedingly long, red-painted fingernails.

'Shut up, you two,' hissed Yuteford, 'or I'll . . .' and he lunged at them and made them run away squealing.

'Sit down, my dears!' urged Mrs Johnson.

Loretta draped herself like a bored ornament across the settee and lit up a cigarette. As she blew a long coil of smoke, her hair, which was beaded in the Afro style, swung like a fringed curtain around her velvet-smooth black face. 'But why,' Effie wondered, 'when she is so beautiful, does she have to wear so much make-up?'

She looked like a painted doll with her red, rouged cheeks and her vivid red lips and her eyes made up like a rainbow.

'We've got a proposition . . .' Yuteford was saying.

'What's a propogician?' asked Seraphina, and she came and stood four square in front of Loretta and folded her arms.

'Little Effie tells me you need someone to housekeep for you, or else you might all be split up and the kids put into care,' said Yuteford.

'Yes, yes, you got it,' nodded Mrs Johnson despairingly.

'Well, I've been putting my mind to the problem, and I suddenly came up with Loretta. She's been singing with our band, and she's just been thrown out of her rooms. Well, you know how difficult it is finding anywhere to live these days, and that's when I had the idea. What if Loretta came to live with you? She could housekeep and cook in exchange for living in, and that way we would kill two birds with one stone. What do you think?'

Mrs Johnson looked helplessly at Effie. Effie dropped her eyes and looked at the ground. It was not at all the sort of person she had in mind.

'I suppose we could think about it,' said Mrs Johnson cautiously.

Then they all stared at Loretta. Loretta puffed on her cigarette and blew a smoke circle into the air as if she didn't care twopence what they thought.

'So you don't think it's a bad proposition,' grinned Yuteford.

'What's a propogician?' demanded Seraphina.

'I must discuss it with the children,' said Mrs Johnson, finally. 'Come again in a couple of days and we'll let you know.'

After Yuteford and Loretta had left, Mrs Johnson asked her children, 'Well, what do you think?'

'Her fingernails are too long,' said Jackson.

'That's 'cos she's a witch,' said Seraphina.

'Her hands don't look as if they've done much washing up,' agreed Mrs Johnson, 'but would she be any help to us at all?'

They all looked at Effie. 'She smokes,' said Effie and burst into tears. Friday had just not been her day at all.

That night when Effie tucked Seraphina up in bed, Seraphina gave her sister an extra fierce hug. 'Effie,' she whispered fearfully, 'what is a propogician?'

'It's a sort of plan,' explained Effie. 'That's all.'

'Oh,' murmured Seraphina, a little disappointed, 'I have lots of plans. Are they propogicians too?'

'I expect so,' replied Effie patting her down. 'Sleep tight.'

The following Tuesday, Loretta moved in. No one really wanted her, but they had no choice. The lady from the Social Services had called round again. 'Well?' she had intoned in a voice which demanded answers.

Mrs Johnson lowered her eyes. She had no answers. None of which were satisfactory, at any rate. It was Effie who spoke firmly.

'We've found someone. A cousin.' (That was a lie, but Effie argued to herself that it was only a little lie, because if Loretta married Yuteford, and she did cling on to his arm most of the time, then she could be a cousin by marriage.) 'She's going to move in with us right away.'

So that was that. Mrs Johnson and the children looked at Effie, amazed, but she didn't look at them. Her chin was firm, and they knew she had made up her mind to it.

'I'm so pleased, my dear,' beamed the lady from the Social Services. She looked genuinely pleased. 'We always try to keep a family together if we possibly can. I'll call by again in a fortnight or so to see how you're getting on.'

So, Loretta moved in. Effie waited for life to change. It did and it didn't. Jackson had to give up his room and move into a corner of Effie and Seraphina's room. He was furious. 'Why should I give up my room?' he fumed, as he tugged down his football posters from the walls.

'It's better than moving home altogether, isn't it?' retorted Effie.

With Loretta moving in, Jackson's room was transformed. It became a boudoir of satin cushions, lacy covers, drawers overflowing with fancy underwear, cupboards bulging with more clothes than Effie thought was possible to wear in a lifetime; and she moved in a proper dressing-table and mirror on which she arranged all her make-up – her row upon row of lipsticks and blushers and eye colours; of bottles of cleansers and moisturisers and toners and night creams and day creams and hand creams, leg creams, eye-wrinkle creams and vein creams; and hair sprays, body sprays, underarm sprays and *eau de cologne* sprays. To go into her room was like going into a world of silk and satin and scent. The smell pervaded the house, and would have been quite pleasant were it not all overlayed with a haze of cigarette smoke which wove itself into all the fabrics and carpets and into the very clothes she wore.

But when were things going to change in Effie's life? When would Loretta take over some of the jobs as promised so that Effie could go and play with her friends? When would Loretta share the housework or help with dressing Mrs Johnson?

The trouble was, Effie was too good at her job. Too good at coping. By the time Loretta had thought of doing something, Effie had already done it. By the time Loretta woke up in the morning, Effie had already washed and dressed her mother, already made the breakfast and got her brother and sister ready for school, already done the hundred little things that need doing in a home. By the time

Loretta wandered into the kitchen in her fluffy pink dressing-gown and her furry, pussy-cat slippers, and lit up her first cigarette of the day, Effie and the children had already gone to school.

Mrs Johnson watched helplessly from her wheelchair. A great void opened up inside her. Loretta wasn't going to be of any help to anyone. She watched in despair as the girl stubbed out her cigarettes into saucers, put off the washing-up and never seemed to notice the dust building up on all the surfaces.

In the middle of the night, when Mrs Johnson called out to be turned over, all her fears tumbled out. 'Oh, Effie darling, what's to be done?'

In the middle of the night, when the human spirit can drop so low, mother and daughter hugged each other for comfort. 'Is there no one else, Mum, who can come and look after us? Don't you know anyone?'

'If only my sister . . . if only Janice . . .'

'Aunty Janice?' exclaimed Effie wonderingly. 'I remember her!' How could she have forgotten, she thought. She wasn't even on her list. 'Why don't we see Aunty Janice any more?' asked Effie. 'Where is she?'

'We had a silly quarrel, such a silly quarrel . . . oh, when I think of it now . . . It was about your dad, oh years ago, and I told her not to bother coming to our house again.

So she didn't, and we were both too proud to make it up. She doesn't even know I'm ill . . .' Mrs Johnson gulped to a halt with tears in her eyes.

Effie tried to remember Aunty Janice. She had the vaguest picture of a rather severe woman who rarely smiled, but who wasn't unkind; she had once bought her a red, blue and green check dress which Seraphina was now wearing. Yes, yes, she remembered now.

'Where does she live?' asked Effie eagerly. A thought was growing inside her. What if . . . what if Aunty Janice could come and live with them?

'I'm not sure,' wailed her mother. 'It was Coventry, but she could have moved. She never married, had no ties, she could have gone anywhere – even back to Jamaica.'

'Oh.' Effie felt disappointment flooding over her. Just when she thought Aunty Janice might be their one true hope. 'But you must have some address,' she persisted.

'In the sideboard, Effie. If there's any address, it will be in the right-hand drawer of the sideboard.'

Everything got thrown into the right-hand drawer of the sideboard. It was stuffed so full, Effie could hardly open it. There were letters and postcards dating back years, as well as old bills and receipts and shopping coupons and tokens for special offers, and photographs, scattered like dead leaves, interweaving everything, and each one that Effie lifted up and examined, took her backwards and forwards in time. There was a picture of her mother when young, laughing with a group of her friends; there she was again, looking more serious as she held a young baby in her arms.

'Is that me?' asked Effie holding it up for her mother to see. It was. There was Jackson, in his football kit and there was Seraphina crawling on the grass. There was one of Dad. Effie looked at it silently, then pushed it to the back of the drawer without any comment. Suddenly . . . there was one . . . she pulled it out hurriedly. It was of a little girl of about five years old, wearing a red, blue and green check dress. Was it she, Effie? Or was it Seraphina? And who was the rather, bosomy lady who solemnly held her hand and stared out into the camera with large, soft eyes. 'Mum?' Effie held out the photograph for identification.

Her mother nodded her head sadly. 'Yes, darling, that's Aunty Janice holding your hand. She was very, very fond of you. She would have taken you away with her if I'd let her. "Any time you're fed up with Effie, give her to me," she would say.'

Effie looked back into the eyes which met hers in the photograph. 'Well then,' she thought. 'If she loves me, then she's bound to help us.'

Another faint memory stirred in the back of her mind. 'Did Aunty Janice sing?'

'She never stopped singing. We called her the songbird, in our family. She was the heart and soul of the church choir. Some said she could have been a professional, but she just said, "I sing to be happy, not to make money."' Mrs Johnson's voice was soft with memories.

'I remember her singing!' exclaimed Effie delightedly. 'She sang to me, didn't she?'

'Oh, yes. Whenever she stayed you made her sing you to sleep. She could never get away. "More, more!" you would cry.'

'She looks like you,' said Effie, and in her head she thought, 'I must find Aunty Janice. We'll be fine if she comes and looks after us. I know we will.'

It took time to find a letter with an address, but at last, after her head was aching with pouring over old letters, she found one from her Aunty Janice. The address was simple. 14, Rufford Road, Coventry. That was all. 'I'm going to write to her,' said Effie. 'She'll come.'

Next morning before school, Effie rose from her bed even earlier than usual. She had already planned a letter to Aunty Janice in her head. She would write it now and post it on her way to school. It said:

Dear Aunty Janice,

  I am your niece, Epiphany Victoria Johnson.

You once bought me a red, green and blue check dress. Now that I've grown out of it, Seraphina wears it. When I was little you used to sing to me and I would ask for more.

I am writing to ask if you would come and live with us and look after Mum. She has been ill and is now unable to walk. If we can't find someone to look after us, me, Jackson and Seraphina will have to go into care.

Please come. Mum would like to be your friend again.

Love from
Effie

Effie expected a reply the very next day. She waited and waited, but it didn't come the next day, or the day after, or the day after that. One week and two weeks went by and then Effie stopped counting, and still no letter came.

'What are you looking so gloomy for, little Effie?' asked Yuteford when he came to call for Loretta.

'Nothing,' grunted Effie, feeling angry inside. Why couldn't Yuteford see that Loretta was no good? Why didn't he realise that since Loretta had moved in, she had only made more work for Effie not less. But when she saw Yuteford's kind, concerned face, she couldn't be cross with him for long.

'I just had a disappointment,' she sighed.

'Oh, little Effie,' murmured Yuteford lifting her up on to his knee with a sympathetic hug. 'What's the matter?'

'Effie didn't get into the school play,' said Seraphina knowingly.

'That's not the reason,' muttered Effie furiously, wriggling off Yuteford's knee.

'T'is so,' agreed Jackson. 'She's always in the school play.'

'Yeh, well, I'm bored by it now. I'm only ever a silly old shepherd or something.'

'Effie wants to be an angel,' cried Seraphina stoutly. She often hit the nail on the head without realising it.

'I do not!' retorted Effie, embarrassed that her secret should be known.

'Anyway, angels are white, ain't they?' snorted Jackson.

'That's not what the matter is,' bellowed Effie.

'Hey, hey! Calm down.' Yuteford caught Effie's arm and wouldn't allow her to storm off. 'If there's something up, you can tell me.'

So Effie told him. Not that Seraphina and Jackson were right about how much she wanted to be in the play; nor the bit about how she missed the audition because of Jackson throwing trainers on the roof; she didn't tell him how much she wanted to be an angel, that she would give an arm and a leg to be an angel. No, she didn't tell him that. No one knew that, not even her mum. She only told him about her Aunty Janice, and how she and her mum weren't friends any more; how she had written to her aunty to try and make it up, but never got a reply. 'I thought it would be very good if Aunty Janice and Mum made it up. I mean, they are sisters!' said Effie.

'You know what, Effie!' exclaimed Yuteford, his face brightening up with a good idea. 'Me and the Band are going to Coventry next weekend. I could look her up.'

Effie felt a surge of hope and excitement rush through her. 'Oh, Yuteford! Please let me go with you,' she begged.

They decided not to tell Mrs Johnson about trying to find Aunty Janice. They didn't want to raise her hopes. All they said was that Yuteford wanted to give Effie a treat by going with the band to Coventry for the weekend.

'I'll have her back pronto by six o'clock Sunday evening,' Yuteford promised. 'Loretta will look after you O.K., won't she?'

Mrs Johnson didn't like to express her doubts about Loretta but she did agree enthusiastically to Effie going with them.

'Yes, Yuteford,' she said. 'Take her with you, and make sure you give her a good time. She deserves a break.'

So next Saturday morning early, a battered van, all painted up in yellow and blue with the names 'Down Town Rats' daubed all over it, came splattering up to the front door. All the children in the street gathered round enviously as little Effie was helped inside. Jackson had wanted to go too and made a big fuss.

'It's not fair!' he wailed at the top of his voice. 'Why should Effie go and not me?'

'Another time, Jackson,' shouted Yuteford firmly, then the van door was slammed shut.

They couldn't guess what a long, tedious day it was going to be. It started off so cheerfully. They sang songs all the way down the motorway and were only a few miles away from Coventry when, suddenly, the van spluttered, choked and wheezed.

'Oh no!' exclaimed Yuteford gazing in dismay at the dashboard. 'All the red lights have come on!'

'What does that mean?' asked Effie.

'It means breakdown!' everyone groaned.

'This could make us late for our gig,' cried the drummer.

It did make them late. Very, very late. By the time they had walked to a telephone, waited for the breakdown van, got towed to a garage, waited two hours to get back on the road again, they were racing against time to make the show that night.

It had all been too much for little Effie. As the van finally sped down the main road into Coventry, she was sound asleep.

'I'm going to have to take little Effie straight

to her aunty's,' muttered Yuteford. 'Let's hope she's there.' He checked the map, and drove through a twist of suburbs until they reached 14 Rufford Road. Then he jumped out of the van, raced up to the front door and hammered loudly on it. An enormously fat lady opened the door and glared at him. 'Yes?' she intoned, her voice heavy with disapproval as she noted the battered van parked outside the house.

'Are you Miss Janice Williams?' asked Yuteford.

'Nope,' came the blunt reply. 'She's busy.'

He could hear the piano playing inside and the sound of gospel singing.

'We're in the middle of a practice. If you're selling something, you'd better come back another time.' She attempted to shut the door.

'Hang on, hang on a minute, missus,' said Yuteford firmly. 'I've brought her a very important person who she won't want to miss.' He dashed back to the van and lifted the sleeping Effie out in his arms and carried her tenderly up the path to the astonished lady. He pushed past her and went into the living-room and stood before the lady at the piano.

'Are you Miss Janice Williams?'

'I am,' she said, rising defensively.

'This is Effie Johnson. I'm in a rush. We're late for a gig. Sorry I can't stop to explain. She'll tell you when she wakes up. I'll be round

tomorrow at midday to collect her. Right?'
Then he slid Effie on to the sofa and ran from
the house.

The St Lucia Gospel Choir turned open-
mouthed and gazed with amazement at the
sleeping child. 'Who is she?' asked one. 'Isn't
she an angel!' murmured another. 'All sleeping
children look like angels,' retorted a third who
seemed to know these things.

'She's my niece, Epiphany Victoria Johnson,'
murmured Aunty Janice softly. 'Ladies, the
choir practice is over for tonight.'

When Effie awoke, she woke without
opening her eyes. She lay listening, feeling that
she was still half asleep and probably
dreaming. She dreamt she was lying on the
couch in her Aunty Janice's house in Coventry.
She couldn't see her aunty, but she could hear
her singing somewhere. Her voice was low and
soft and sweet, and she sang Effie's favourite
song: 'Hush little baby don't say a word,
Momma's gonna buy you a mocking bird, and
if that mocking bird don't sing, Momma's
gonna buy you a diamond ring . . .'

Then she frowned in a puzzled sort of way.
You don't usually smell things in dreams, and
Effie could smell hot buttered toast. The smell
made her so hungry that she opened her eyes
and sat bolt upright and shouted, 'I'm hungry!'

'Are you, my precious?' A woman appeared
in the doorway. She was trim and neat with

iron-grey hair tied back tightly into a severe knot at the back of her neck.

Her face had been moulded over the years into the solemn creases of those who don't smile much, and yet her serious dark eyes were warm with affection and the corners of her mouth turned up gently into a reserved smile.

'Ah, Effie! At last you're awake.' She came over almost awkwardly and knelt on the floor by the sofa. She didn't kiss her, but smoothed her head with a light hand. 'So, it's my little Effie,' she murmured, 'and not so little now. Last time you lay on my sofa, you hardly reached down to the middle of it, now look at you!'

Effie craned up her neck and saw that her feet nearly touched the bottom of the sofa.

'Are you my Aunty Janice?' she asked.

'I surely am!' Aunty Janice's smile got bigger.

'So, you didn't go back to Jamaica,' cried Effie gleefully. 'You still live at 14 Rufford Road.'

'I do,' chuckled Aunty Janice. Yes, she actually chuckled when she saw the incredulous delight on Effie's face.

'Then you can come and live with us and look after Mum, and me and Jackson and Seraphina won't be taken into care and all split up, and Loretta can go away and . . .'

'Just a minute! Hold your horses!' Aunty Janice put her arms round the girl who was quivering with excitement.

'What's all this about me looking after you?'

'Don't you know?' Effie's voice turned to desperation. 'Don't you know? Didn't you get my letter?'

'No, precious. I didn't get your letter, but look, let's have breakfast. The Lord only knows when you last ate. Tell me about it over breakfast.'

Effie ate everything which was put before her: a large bowl of porridge, fried egg, beans on toast, lots more toast with lashings of honey and finally she managed to swallow down a banana on top of all that because she loved bananas. Then Effie told her everything.

Aunty Janice listened in almost total silence, except when she said, 'I see,' from time to time, in a very grave voice.

When Effie had finished Aunty Janice said, 'I'm just going to pack myself an overnight bag. I think I'd better come back with you and see the situation for myself.'

It was a bit of a squeeze. Aunty Janice sat up in front with Yuteford, while Effie sat on someone's knee in the back.

The Down Town Rats had had a great gig and they were full of high spirits. They sang all the way back and even Aunty Janice joined in. This time, there were no breakdowns or holdups of any sort, and within a couple of hours the van turned the corner into Effie's road.

Suddenly, Yuteford braked urgently, and everyone jerked forward.

'Hey, man!' they grumbled at the back. 'What's going on!' They all turned and craned to see through the front windscreen. There was a low gasp of alarm. An ambulance was parked outside Effie's house with its blue light silently flashing. A cluster of curious neighbours hung around the gate.

'Oh, Good Lord help us!' exclaimed Aunty Janice. 'What's happening?'

They watched a stretcher being gently eased through the front door followed by Loretta who was weeping noisily.

'Mum, Mum, Mum.' The van was full of the sound of Effie screaming and struggling to get out. Someone opened the van doors and they all tumbled out into the road. Effie tried to rush up to the stretcher, but Yuteford grabbed her. 'Hush, hush, little Effie. Just hold on a minute while I go see what's up. Here, stay with your Aunty Janice.' He thrust her firmly into Aunty Janice's protective arms.

Now the woman from the Social Services came out holding hands with Jackson and Seraphina. The children's faces were as blank as statues until they saw Yuteford. Then they burst out crying, and Jackson broke free of the lady and charged headfirst at Yuteford kicking and pummelling him furiously.

'See!' he yelled. 'You shouldn't have taken

Effie away from us. Loretta didn't know how to help Mum out of the wheelchair and she fell. Now she's going to hospital and we're all to be taken into care. I hate you. It's all your fault.'

Then Seraphina came up whimpering and took his hand. 'Please don't let them take us away, Yuteford.'

Then they saw Effie and ran crying to their elder sister who grabbed them both and shouted, 'No one's sending us away. No one.'

All at once, Aunty Janice took charge. She marched right into the middle of the rumpus. First she went into the ambulance and bent over her sister. There were whispered reassurances and hugs and kisses. When she got out, the ambulance drove away, and Aunty Janice walked forthrightly up to the lady from the Social Services.

'I think we should all go inside and discuss this,' she said firmly.

Yuteford and Loretta took charge of the children. 'Hey, Jackson!' shouted Yuteford. 'Wanna trip in the van with the band?'

'Me too, Yuteford. Me too!' cried Seraphina.

As Effie watched her aunt and the social worker go into the house, the terror inside Effie's soul began to subside. Just before Aunty Janice shut the front door behind her, she turned to look at Effie, then blew her a kiss. Then she knew. 'Everything's gonna be all right!' she breathed. 'Everything's gonna be all right.'

That night, the children clustered round Aunty Janice in their pyjamas. Effie said, 'Will you sing to us, Aunty?'

'Get to bed then, all of you,' she ordered, 'and I'll sit where you can all hear me, and sing you something.'

The children flew to their beds – even Jackson – and snuggled down under the blankets till only their ears were peeking up.

'Hush little baby don't say a word, Momma's gonna buy you a mocking bird . . .' As Aunty Janice's rich, deep voice filled the house, Effie felt herself slipping away into the deepest sleep she had known in a long time.

The carols echoed through the school. Everyone was in the hall rehearsing for the nativity play. Even Effie. Though she had missed the auditions and didn't get a part, everybody had to be in the play in one way or another, and Mrs Freeman said that Effie should sing in the choir.

'Will we get to dress up as angels, in the choir?' asked Effie hopefully. If she couldn't be an angel, she could look like one, perhaps.

But Mrs Freeman said, 'Sorry, Effie! Everyone can't be angels, you know. We haven't got enough cardboard. Just you wear your best dress.'

Effie sighed with disappointment and took her place in the choir. As she sang, she watched her friend Carlene, who was the angel Gabriel. Carlene looked beautiful; the perfect angel, with her long, golden hair and her wide, blue eyes.

'I wish . . . I wish . . .' whispered Effie to herself. 'I wish I looked like Carlene, *then perhaps they'd let me be an angel.'*

'Penny for your thoughts, Effie!' Aunt Janice challenged her over supper. Effie was fiddling with her food and daydreaming. She was the Angel Gabriel standing up there on stage at the top of the steps, saying in a loud, clear voice which everyone could hear from the back of the hall, 'Behold! I bring you glad tidings!'

'Nothing, Aunty!' murmured Effie. 'I was only wondering what to wear for the school play.'

'I'm wearing my lamb's outfit, aren't I, Mum!' boasted Seraphina going over to her mother. Mrs Johnson, who was back from hospital and feeling generally more relaxed, was carefully sewing Seraphina's costume and had just stitched on the tail.

'Did you see my crown, Effie?' cried Jackson. 'Just you wait! It's gold and fixed inside a green turban with lots of jewels all over it.'

'Bits of paper, you mean,' snorted Seraphina in a mean voice.

'Oh, shut up!' shouted Jackson.

'Children, children! You'll be sent to wash

your mouths out with soap if I hear any more bad language,' threatened Aunt Janice. 'Eat up now, or you won't be fit for the play tomorrow.'

Yes, the nativity play was the very next day, and the very next day in class, Mrs Freeman looked worried and agitated. Carlene, the Angel Gabriel, had gone down with chicken pox!

'This is terrible!' she had wailed in the staff room. 'Who can I get to play the part at such short notice?'

When she stood before her class she looked at all the children carefully. 'Who here knows the part of the Angel Gabriel?' she asked. 'Is there anyone here who hasn't got a part and could do the Angel Gabriel tonight?'

There was silence. Everybody shuffled and looked nervous. Nobody spoke up. Then suddenly, a voice from the back said firmly, 'I could do it, Mrs Freeman. I know the lines.'

'Effie!' exclaimed her teacher. 'All right, Effie. Come and see me at breaktime and we'll see what you can do!'

Effie was running.

'Stop running, Effie. I got a stitch,' wailed Seraphina.

Effie was running.

'Stop running, Effie, my shoe's rubbing,' grumbled Jackson.

45

Effie was running, running, running. Running home from school. She wanted to tell the world. Shout it out all over the universe. But she didn't tell anyone yet. Not till she'd told her mother first. She ran and ran, with Seraphina and Jackson tagging along behind.

'Mum!' she shrieked as she burst in through the door. 'Mum! I'm gonna be an angel!'

'What?' cried her mother in amazement.

'Hallelujah!' exclaimed Aunty Janice clapping her hands.

'You – an angel!' sneered Jackson, kicking off his shoes.

'Oooh, Effie! Will you wear a white dress with wings and a halo?' breathed Seraphina enviously. 'I wish . . . I wish . . .'

'Are you going to come and see me, Mum?' asked Effie.

''Course I am. Wild horses wouldn't stop me.'

'You don't need wild horses, just me!' laughed Aunt Janice.

Aunt Janice took Mum to see the play. She pushed her all the way to the school in her wheelchair. And weren't they proud when little Effie climbed up the three steps on stage and stood there taller than anyone in her long, white dress with a gold halo strapped to her head and silver wings pinned to her shoulder blades. And weren't they proud when she spoke her lines so loud and clear that everyone could hear at the back. Effie didn't make a single mistake.

'I think she was born for the part,' whispered Aunty Janice.

'She was, she was!' agreed Mrs Johnson.

And there was Jackson all dressed up, magnificent in shining robes and his gold and green turban crown, and there was Seraphina in her lamb's outfit.

Afterwards, as everyone was clapping as loud as thunder, Seraphina came and stood proudly next to her beautiful sister. 'Effie,' she whispered. 'When I grow up, I'm going to be an angel like you.'

2

The Private World of Rajiv Ray

Everyone knew that there was something different about Rajiv from the very first day he arrived at school as a new boy.

It wasn't just that he looked odd, with his owlish spectacles, his wild, black straggly hair and his long, lanky out-of-control limbs, it was the way he behaved. Rajiv acted as though there was no one else in the world except him.

He could be in a classroom packed with gabbling children, yet seem completely alone; he could be spoken to over and over again yet not seem to hear; and he had the habit of looking straight at you yet not seem to see. Meanwhile, he would grunt and sniff and clear his throat all the time so that once a teacher complained that it was like having a piglet in the class.

It was as though Rajiv existed on another planet, his mind always in some other world. And when he wasn't staring into space, he was reading. Rajiv read books as if his life depended on it. He was never without a book, even in the playground, even when he went to the lavatory. In fact he would spend most of his time during playtime, locked in the lavatory so that he could read without being disturbed. Rajiv read anything and everything. He read all the books in the school library and kept asking for more. And not all Rajiv's books were in English either. Some were in a long, curly, wriggly script which made the other children hoot with laughter.

'Hey, Rajiv! Did a spider crawl all over your books or something?' they taunted. In fact the intensity with which Rajiv crouched over his books somehow reminded Ben, the boy who sat next to him, of a spider devouring a fly.

If Rajiv was crazy about books, Ben was crazy about football. He was never without his football and every spare minute, both in and out of school, he was kicking, heading, dribbling, scoring either alone or with his friends.

Yet Ben was the only boy who could be called Rajiv's friend. Rajiv didn't seem to need or want friends. When he first arrived the other children teased him unmercifully but Rajiv just frowned vaguely and ignored them as though they were no more troublesome than a cluster of sparrows. But this wasn't good enough for the children so one of the bigger boys picked a fight and bloodied Rajiv's nose. It was then that Ben had bravely intervened, shooed them off and offered Rajiv his hanky. Rajiv didn't even thank him, but pressed the hanky to his streaming nose, picked up his book which had been tossed round the playground and carried on reading.

Perhaps the bullies were scared by the blood or perhaps it was because Rajiv didn't tell on them, but they left him alone after that.

The next day Rajiv returned Ben's hanky to him. It had been washed, folded, ironed and was spotlessly clean.

Rajiv's house was just round the corner from Ben's but though Ben was allowed to go to school on his own because it was only five minutes away and there were no main roads to cross, Rajiv never walked alone. Every morning he came out with Sumi, his tall, long-plaited older sister, who would see him right up to the school gates, and then go on to the local comprehensive further up the road; and every afternoon he was met by an old, old Indian man wearing Indian style dress with tunic, waistcoat and white cotton pyjamas. Ben thought this must be Rajiv's grandfather, though Rajiv never talked about him, or his sister or his parents or anyone else in the world.

On their walks to school, Ben would often try to talk to Rajiv. He'd ask him excitedly,

'Hey, did you see the football match on telly last night! Wasn't it brilliant?' But Rajiv would throw him a puzzled stare as if he had never heard of football or even of television, and carry on grunting. So Ben talked to Sumi. She was nice and chatty even though she was much older, and Ben thought she was beautiful with her long, black shiny plaits which swung as she walked.

Often a boy from Sumi's school hung around the top of the road and joined them. It was Gary. He was sixteen, the same age as Sumi with teasing blue eyes and brown curly hair. He was always making them laugh. Sumi liked him, Ben could see that but she seemed uneasy, too. So she would march ahead with Rajiv, her long plaits swinging even more energetically, forcing Gary to follow behind with Ben. Ben didn't mind as they both loved football.

One morning Gary had just joined them when a white Rolls Royce pulled up silently alongside them. An automatic window purred as it slid down and Sumi and Rajiv stopped to speak to the people inside. The voices sounded angry, and then suddenly the door was flung open. Sumi and Rajiv got in and were driven away.

'Who was that?' gasped Ben, deeply impressed. He thought only queens and millionaires rode round in Rolls Royces.

Gary looked upset and kicked a tree. 'That's Sumi and Rajiv's aunt and uncle. They live with them. Haven't you seen?'

Ben had once seen the Rolls Royce driving out of Rajiv's house and it had seemed mysterious, but then everything about Rajiv was mysterious. The biggest mystery of all was his house. Ben was amazed that anyone should want to live in such a place, it was so huge and gloomy. Most of these Victorian houses had been knocked down long ago and rows of little modern houses had been built in their place, like the house Ben lived in. Somehow Rajiv's house remained, a vast conglomeration of pitched roofs, clusters of chimneys, long, staring windows and wrought-iron balconies. Nearby, a huge old oak tree stood on guard like a giant watchman. High up, in the very tops of the branches, dozens of cawing, black crows congregated like a coven of witches, their heavy, shiny bodies tipping to breaking point the slender boughs.

Ben knew the house and grounds well from the outside. Before Rajiv moved in, the house had been empty for nearly a year. As it had the biggest garden in the neighbourhood, he and his friends often came in to kick a football on the weedy, gravelly drive in front of the house, or to play hide and seek in and out of the tangled, overgrown shrubbery. But the place had always made Ben feel a little uneasy.

Perhaps it was the way the large, dusty windows seemed to stare out at them with black eyes, and if they tried to peer inside, they saw nothing except darkness. It was as though the house was only a shell incorporating nothing but darkness stretching away as endlessly as space.

Even when Rajiv moved in, the house didn't lose its mystery. In fact it still continued to look uninhabited. Nobody came to paint the crumbling woodwork or to hang curtains in the windows or to cut back the weeds.

'Where are Rajiv and Sumi's parents then?' asked Ben.

'In India,' Gary told him. 'Their grandfather looks after Rajiv and Sumi, and their aunt and uncle, when they can be bothered. They're so strict. She's not allowed to talk to any boy out of school, that's why, when they saw me they made them get into the car. I bet they'll marry her off to some stinking-rich businessman back in India . . .and then . . .' Gary's voice choked a little. He strode on ahead managing to call back, 'See yer, Ben!'

'See yer,' replied Ben thoughtfully. He began to think of Sumi as a fairy-tale princess being whisked away like a damsel in distress.

When he got to school, Rajiv was already at his desk grunting, sniffing and clearing his throat as he crouched over a book about dinosaurs. Ben knew that it would be useless to ask him any questions, so he just said, 'You lucky thing, getting to ride in a Rolls Royce!' Rajiv didn't reply.

After that they hardly saw Gary, as he left school and went to work for his dad who ran a local garden centre. So Rajiv and Sumi went walking to school as usual with Ben joining them too. Once, after school, Gary, perhaps by accident, perhaps on purpose, bumped into Ben and slipped him a note. 'Give this to Sumi, will yer?' he asked. 'But keep it a secret, mind!'

Sumi sent one back in return, and Ben became their messenger.

Then one day, neither Rajiv nor Sumi were on the road to school. They weren't there the next day or the next. Once, as Ben was passing the top of Rajiv's driveway down to the house, he saw the white Rolls Royce standing at the front door. He lingered to see if he might catch a glimpse of anyone, but he didn't. Then Gary was waiting again for him outside school. 'You haven't brought a note for me for days. What's happening?' he asked anxiously. 'Where's Sumi? Her mates say she hasn't been at school.'

'I don't know,' shrugged Ben. 'Rajiv hasn't been in school either.'

'Hmmm!' grunted Gary, and stomped off with his shoulders down and his hands in his pockets. 'Let me know if you hear anything!' he muttered.

Ben heard something the next day. His

teacher called him over. 'Ben! We have a message from Rajiv's grandfather. Rajiv hasn't been well and he's worried he'll get behind in his work. You live close by, and he's a friend of yours, isn't he? Please drop these books in to him on your way home.'

Ben nodded but felt suddenly uneasy. He realised that he had never gone up to the front door of the house before. Never called for Rajiv to come and play.

'You don't mind, do you?' asked his teacher noticing his reluctance.

'No, miss,' Ben assured her. How could he explain the rush of anxiety he felt at the prospect of walking down that long drive and knocking at the huge front door?

So when school was over, Ben set off with Rajiv's books and soon found himself standing at the old stone gates.

It was a still day as if everything held its breath. Not a leaf stirred, nor a blade of grass trembled in the undergrowth. Even the black crows seemed to have abandoned the tree that day. Silence and loneliness overwhelmed him. He hesitated and would have turned back but for wondering how Rajiv and Sumi were.

So he began walking down the drive, his eye fixed determinedly on the huge front door sheltering within the crumbling, ivy-clad portico.

There was still no sign of life and not a breath

of sound, and Ben wondered if he should just leave the books on the step and go. Then he thought this might seem rude and unfriendly so he tugged at the old rusty ring which protruded through the ivy. When at last the echoes of the clanging and jangling had died away and still no one had come, Ben turned away with relief and began to retreat.

'Oh, Ben! How good of you to call!'

Ben turned in amazement. He hadn't heard the front door open, and now he found himself staring into the dark, friendly face of Rajiv's grandfather. His deep brown eyes twinkled shiny as conkers as he said, 'Come in, come in, I'm so glad you came,' and he stood aside to wave Ben into the house.

Ben crossed over the threshold and stood sightless for a moment in the gloom of the house. Was this the nothingness he had imagined so often? Yet now the afternoon sun thrust its way in behind him and fell like a great golden pool on the floor of the hall. Some of the beams flew up the stairs in front and struck a large glistening object on the landing and seemed to set it on fire.

It was a statue. Ben had never seen anything like it before. It was a dancing figure of glittering bronze which seemed to come alive in the sunlight. But this was no ordinary dancer. This was a dancing god with four long arms which bent and stretched in this direction then in that direction; the wrists twisted with upturned palms or gracefully drooped with fingers closing like lotus petals; the legs lifted, knees bending, feet stamping, and in such a strange mixture of gestures and expressions, the statue seemed to throb to an unheard rhythm.

Then the door closed behind him. The golden pool of sunlight vanished. The dancer disappeared.

'Where's Rajiv?' whispered Ben.

'He's in his room,' replied the old man. 'Take the books up to him, it will do him good to see another human being. Please.' The grandfather could see that Ben wanted to leave. He had edged towards the door.

'Well, I mustn't stay long. I'm playing football later,' Ben excused himself.

'Stay, just a little while,' begged the grandfather. 'You see it's not so much that Rajiv is ill. It's that he's lonely now that Sumi's gone.'

'Sumi! Gone? Where?' gasped Ben. Somehow his heart dropped to his boots.

'It was decided. She is nearly seventeen. She is ready to be married. Her aunt and uncle suggested it and her parents called her home to India, so it can be arranged.'

'Has she gone to India to be married?' cried Ben in dismay. He remembered Gary's words.

'Yes, yes,' sighed the old man. 'It is our

custom, you know, but poor Rajiv! Sumi was his best friend, and he misses her so much he has refused to go out since she left.'

As they climbed the stairs to Rajiv's bedroom, they passed the dancing god who, now that Ben's eyes had adjusted to the gloom, seemed to beckon him to join the dance.

'That is Shiva! Lord Shiva!' smiled the old man noticing Ben's interest. 'Rajiv and Sumi loved him. He dances the dance of the Cosmos. He creates the world with his dance and destroys the demons beneath his stamping feet. Sumi and Rajiv, they would dance too and play such games. They both missed India very much, you see, and Shiva reminded them . . .' his voice trailed away.

Suddenly a peal of laughter broke through the darkness.

'Sumi! Wasn't that Sumi?' cried Ben.

'No, no, it is just Rajiv playing. They played such games . . .they missed their parents, they missed their friends, and most of all, they just missed being back home. They would both pretend they were there. They imagined that their friends came to visit them. Sometimes I can hear them playing, and it's as if they have brought all their friends over from India – just magicked them into the house! Isn't that silly!' The old man laughed softly.

There was another peal of laughter and the sound of excited chattering.

'She's there now, Sumi! I can hear them both!' cried Ben. They stood outside a bedroom door.

The grandfather knocked loudly. 'Rajiv! Ben is here with some of your school books. He wants to see you.'

The laughter in the room stopped as suddenly as if a switch had been turned off. The old man pushed the door open. Ben stood staring in amazement. The room was quite empty. He couldn't even see Rajiv at first. All he could see were books. Books were everywhere; they were strewn across the bed, piled in tottering piles on the floor, tumbled along bookshelves tossed everywhere so that there was barely a space to walk.

Then he heard the familiar sound of grunting, sniffing and the clearing of a throat. 'Rajiv?' Ben called out timidly.

The old man nodded encouragingly. 'Stay. Play,' he said and quietly left the room. Ben moved closer to the sound of sniffing and grunting. Then he saw him. Rajiv was on the floor behind one of the tall piles of books, crouched over a particularly large, ancient crumbling book, with the same spidery script Ben had seen in some of his other books.

Ben knelt down on the floor beside him. 'What are you reading?' he asked. The response came, but it seemed like an age before Rajiv looked up – looking but not seeing – as if really asleep in the grip of a dream. His stare was black, bottomless, impenetrable, but as he went on gazing into Ben's eyes, a tiny glimmering tear welled up, trembling. He blinked it away and focused. Now he looked at Ben and saw him. Still he said nothing, but frowned.

'Are you feeling better? I've brought you some books,' said Ben, not really knowing what else to say. He looked around him wondering if Sumi or some other children might now jump out and the laughter would start all over again.

'I heard Sumi!' Ben said.

'I'm learning how to bring her here!' whispered Rajiv. Suddenly, his eyes glittered sharply like diamonds, sparkling with excitement.

'All I have to do is concentrate. Concentrate so hard that my thoughts – my mind can bring her here to me – and anyone else I want.'

'How?' breathed Ben disbelievingly. 'It's impossible.'

'It isn't, it isn't,' murmured Rajiv, and he returned to his book, hunching even lower over it.

Ben too crouched over the book, wonderingly, fascinated, as Rajiv's finger ran along the strange script accompanied by his muttering incomprehensible sounds. Every now and then Rajiv would lean back on his heels and throw his face upwards with his eyes closed.

Suddenly Ben heard a tinkling laugh behind him. He turned and looked. There was no one there. Rajiv continued reading and running his finger along the line of strange squiggles. He heard another laugh and voices overlapping. Swift as anything, Ben turned and looked again, but there was nothing and no one to be seen. He jumped to his feet, afraid. His almost violent movement knocked the book away from Rajiv, who looked up at him as if he'd been awoken suddenly. He blinked in a confused way.

'What are you doing here?' he asked, as if seeing Ben for the first time.

'I brought you your books,' Ben shouted. He was angry inside. 'I'm going to football now.' He made for the door.

Rajiv leapt to his feet. 'Football?' he asked. 'Like this . . . or like this . . . like this?' He leapt into different football positions as he spoke, kicking and heading an imaginary ball.

'Yes, yes,' laughed Ben, suddenly relaxed. 'Why don't you come,' and he grabbed his arm. 'We need more people to make up the team.'

Rajiv went on kicking and tossing so gracefully that suddenly he seemed to Ben to look like the bronze statue, and his footballing became a dance. Then just as suddenly, he stopped and dropped to the floor, pulling the book back in front of him. His mouth tight shut.

'Bye then,' muttered Ben, and went out of the room.

As he passed the dancing statue of Shiva, Ben heard the tinkling laugh again. He rushed down the stairs and out of the front door without saying goodbye to the old man who he saw emerging out of the shadows.

He didn't stop running till he reached the top of the drive.

'Ben! Did you see her?' It was Gary lingering in the road. 'Is Sumi O.K.?'

Ben looked at him frowning, confused, still angry. 'No. She isn't there.'

'What do you mean "she isn't there"? Where is she then?'

'They've sent her back to India to get married,' Ben told him.

'But . . .'

Gary's head dropped despairingly and he thrust his fist into the palm of his hand.

'I knew it, I knew it!'

'But . . .' Ben tried again.

'But what?' snapped Gary.

'But . . . I . . . ' Ben was going to say, 'I nearly saw her. I heard her . . .' but it seemed ridiculous. Instead he said, 'Rajiv plays a game. He reads a book . . . he . . .'

'What do I care what Rajiv does?' asked Gary impatiently.

'Well, he's trying to bring her back.'

'They'll never let her come back.'

'Not in that way bring her back.' Ben struggled to explain. 'I mean in his imagination. He concentrates so hard, it's as though she's there. I heard her!'

'You what?' exclaimed Gary. 'Don't get funny with me. Either she really is there . . .' His face brightened with hope.

'No, she's not. I know she's gone,' insisted Ben.

'Then you're going off your rocker or something,' cried Gary. 'You shouldn't get too involved. They're different from us. Well, I'm off now,' he added dejectedly. 'See yer!'

'See yer!' echoed Ben.

But though Ben went on his way, when he turned and looked back, Gary hadn't moved. He was leaning up against the tree, his head buried in his arm, as if for a while his whole world had ended.

The next day Rajiv was back at school. He was dropped off in the white Rolls Royce. It caused a big stir among the children and the grown-ups! There were cries of envy. Ben was kicking a football around in the playground. He called out to him, 'Hi, Rajiv!'

But Rajiv just passed by as though he didn't exist. Mischievously, Ben kicked the football hard in Rajiv's direction. It should have hit him on the back but instead, with a movement like quicksilver, Rajiv turned, ducked, and headed it straight back.

By the time Ben had recovered from his shock, Rajiv had disappeared into the classroom.

'Did you see that!' exclaimed a boy. 'Did Rajiv do that?'

'Mmmm!' murmured Ben thoughtfully and followed Rajiv inside.

It was football that afternoon. The boys changed in the cloakrooms. They pulled on brightly striped football shirts and dark blue shorts, and fumbled with the laces on their football boots. They were full of chatter and laughter and fantasies about being great footballers. They could already hear the wild cheering of crowds in their ears as they tumbled out on to the wide, empty, green playing field. Only Rajiv lolled about in uninterested fashion, slowly pulling on his shirt and shorts and taking ages to tie his boot laces. He looked even more gangly and spider-like when he emerged. The last one to leave the cloakroom.

'Come on, Rajiv! We haven't got all day!' bellowed the teacher.

Ben and Stephen were told to pick two teams. They stood side by side taking it in turns to choose, each hoping to get the best players.

There were four boys left now. It was the

same four whom no one really wanted on their team. Rajiv was one of them, the only one who didn't care. He just stood there as if in a dream, his eyes gazing somewhere over the tops of the boys' heads, chewing his lip, grunting, sniffing and clearing his throat.

'Rajiv!' called Ben when it was his turn to choose.

His team gasped. 'Are you mad? Why Rajiv? He's hopeless! He's the worst in the school! You should have chosen Paul or Richard.'

'Rajiv!' Ben called again. Rajiv didn't seem to have heard him the first time. Now he shuffled over and stood on Ben's side, ignoring the outraged looks he received from the others.

'I'm making you goalkeeper, O.K.?' said Ben.

Rajiv shrugged his shoulders and wandered over to stand vaguely between the goal posts.

The teacher blew the whistle. The boys were off. How they ran, kicked, dribbled, manoeuvred, first towards this goal post, then with a sudden surge, a whistle, a free kick, a change of direction and they all surged the other way.

Suddenly a boy got the ball between his feet and was running like the wind. Nearer and nearer he came towards Rajiv's goal post.

'Rajiv! Get ready!' shrieked Ben desperately. Rajiv wasn't even looking. 'Wham,' the ball sailed through the air. Rajiv had time, if only he had been looking, he had time to see it and take action. But no, it almost touched his head and thudded into the net behind him.

'Goal!' shrieked Stephen's team with delight.

'Oh no! Rajiv!' wailed Ben's team in dismay.

'He didn't even try, the dumbhead!' yelled someone furiously.

'Wake up, Rajiv!' roared the teacher. 'Just for once give us your attention!'

But Rajiv was in another world as usual. He carried on dreaming and staring into space, and it wasn't long before another and another and another ball sailed past his head into the goal.

'That'll teach you to pick him for our team. Just because he's your friend,' snorted someone in disgust. 'I just don't understand you. You know he's hopeless.'

'It's not because he's my friend,' protested Ben. 'It's because I saw him do this amazing header in the playground this morning . . . and I thought . . .' he trailed off lamely.

'Well, don't choose him again. EVER!' ordered his friend.

After school, Ben found himself walking not far behind Rajiv and his grandfather. He hung back unwilling to catch up. He was still feeling annoyed with Rajiv for letting him down so badly. Suddenly, coming towards them was Gary. Ben never knew if it was by accident or on purpose that he was there, but when Rajiv saw him, he gave a terrible cry of rage and rushed headfirst into Gary's stomach.

Gary gave a grunt of pain and staggered backwards clutching the furious boy. Rajiv was shouting and yelling. 'It's all your fault; your fault. It's because of you they sent her away. I hate you, I hate you!' With each cry he kicked and headbutted and battled with the astonished young man.

'Hey get off, you maniac!' choked Gary, struggling to free himself. But it was as though Rajiv was possessed by an incredible strength. Nothing would shake him off. The two boys now fell to the ground, their arms lashing out.

The grandfather rushed forward, so did Ben. They both grabbed Rajiv and tried to pull him off. Rajiv still shouted in anguish, tears were streaming down his face.

'If it hadn't been for you . . . I hate you . . . I hate you . . .' he stormed.

'Stop it, Rajiv! Stop it!' cried Ben. 'It won't do any good.'

At last, as if exhausted, Rajiv loosened his hold. 'Why did he behave like that?' cried Ben. 'Why go for Gary?'

'Rajiv's aunt found one of Gary's notes in Sumi's school blazer pocket. That's what made them decide to send her away,' replied the grandfather. 'They were afraid she would make the wrong sort of friends – and Gary, I'm afraid, was definitely seen to be the wrong sort of friend.'

'Then it's my fault, too,' said Ben in a small voice. 'I helped.'

Gary still sat on the ground, his head in his hands. 'I'm sorry, Rajiv. I'm really sorry,' he said softly. 'I miss her.'

'What's done is done, young man. Do not blame yourself,' murmured the grandfather. 'Rajiv is upset. He misses Sumi very much.' Then he turned to Ben. 'Come, Ben. Come with us? Stay and keep Rajiv company for a while?'

'I'll have to go home first and tell my mum,' said Ben. 'I expect I'll be able to come for a while.' At first Ben felt reluctant and didn't really want to go, but the old man gave him such a look of friendship that he couldn't say 'No'.

As Ben left Rajiv and his grandfather at the top of their drive, Gary caught up with him. 'This stuff you said about Rajiv thinking Sumi back here, do you reckon it's true?' he asked.

'I dunno,' sighed Ben. 'I heard laughing. It sounded like Sumi, but it could have been Rajiv. I've never heard him laugh.'

'Tell me if anything like that happens again,' begged Gary.

'What can you do if it does?' asked Ben.

'Nothing, I suppose, but just tell me, O.K.?' Gary looked pale.

'O.K.,' replied Ben, and turned into the gate of his house.

Ben brought his football with him when he returned to Rajiv's house after tea. Somehow he hadn't given up hope. He knew what he had seen, and it was hard to believe that Rajiv's header in the playground that morning had been a fluke. He stood in the crumbling portico now with the football tucked under his arm and stared at the open door. Then he stepped into the hallway following the stream of light and once more saw the dancing god, Shiva, beckoning him up the stairs.

'Hello! I've come!' Ben called out. His voice rang out too loud in the still house and he wished he hadn't.

'Go on up, Ben.' It was the grandfather's voice calling out from somewhere. 'Rajiv is expecting you.'

Leaving the door open as he found it, Ben ran upstairs. He reached Rajiv's door and heard a tinkle of laughter. He thrust open the bedroom door without knocking and defiantly rushed inside.

The room was darkened as the curtains were drawn and none of the late afternoon sun penetrated the gloom. There was the stillness of chaos as though he had arrived seconds after the books had been tossed, the bedspread pulled back, and the piles of magazines had begun to totter. In the middle of the floor was an Indian drum waiting to be played, and then he saw Rajiv standing in a far corner. He was wearing Indian dress, jodhpur-style cotton pyjamas which emphasised his long, thin legs, and a flimsy white tunic which glowed in the darkness. It was like looking at the statue of Shiva. Rajiv stood motionless on one leg, the other raised high in front of him with bent knee. His long arms stretched forward gracefully as if both beckoning and shielding. Movement seemed to flow through him, and yet he was as still as a statue. 'Rajiv!' Ben whispered. At the sound of his voice, Rajiv moved his head, and his eyes followed a line round the wall until they met his gaze, then he sprang on to the other foot.

'Beat the drum, Ben! Beat the drum!' murmured Rajiv. 'Like this . . . and like this . . . and like this . . . and like this . . .' He clapped his hands in a simple rhythm to show Ben.

Ben obeyed. He didn't know why. Suddenly he wanted to join in with Rajiv's game. He knelt before the drum and struck it with his fingers. 'Like this . . . and like this . . . and like this . . . Boom de de . . . Boom de de . . . Boom de de . . . Boom.'

Ben picked up the rhythm and Rajiv began to stamp in time with the beat, twisting and turning and changing his shape to the pulse of the drum.

They went on and on and on with Rajiv now urging him to beat faster and faster. Now his stamping was more fierce and he whirled around with his arms and legs changing his shape with every move. On and on till Ben's fingers ached, and now he grew weary and longed to stop. His beat faltered.

'Keep up, keep up!' urged Rajiv. 'Boom de de . . . Boom de de . . . Boom de de . . .'

'This is boring, Rajiv!' yelled Ben. 'I've had enough of this silly game. I've played your game, now you play mine. Come on! I've brought my football.'

He jumped up and grabbing his football, threw it at Rajiv.

Rajiv caught it with his bare toe and kicked it up and caught it with his heel, then to his other toe and to his heel, to his knee to his head, from this foot then to that foot so that at times it seemed as if he had four heads and four legs. Ben just stood flabbergasted. Then Rajiv just let the ball roll away from him under the bed.

'Beat the drum, Ben! Beat the drum!' Rajiv cried and went on dancing. 'Boom de de . . . Boom de de . . . Boom de de . . . Boom . . .'

Ben felt caught up now in the magic of the rhythm. He had to go back and beat the drum. It beat with his heart, and the panting of his breath, and the blood pumping round his body. He didn't waver, even when he heard the laughter – Sumi's laughter! Even when he heard the tinkle of children's voices, right by his ear, he didn't waver. He went on beating the drum and watching Rajiv dance and dance.

'Beat the drum! Beat the drum!' Rajiv danced and danced. Ben could see his stamping feet and waving arms.

Suddenly the gloom of the room lifted and lifted. A bright light poured in and the four walls stretched away and away and away, disappearing into a vivid, blue, Indian sky and a great, dry, browny-green, parched common. A skyline of sparkling white flat-roofed houses shimmered in the distance, and scattered across the grass in the cooling shade of mango trees, mothers in sarees gossipped and old men smoked their hookahs. There were children playing and barefoot boys yelling merrily as they kicked a football from one end of the common to the other.

'Beat the drum! Beat the drum!' Suddenly, there was Rajiv running across the brown grass to join the footballers. 'I've come to play too!' he shouted.

'And me!' cried Ben. 'Wait for me!' The drumming ceased as he leapt to his feet.

Briefly the vision faded, like a light flickering. 'Beat the drum! Beat the drum!' urged a voice.

As Ben sped across the brown field after Rajiv, he heard the throb of the drum as someone else took over and it beat again.

The ball came his way. He rushed at it and

sent it hurtling towards a group of boys. They all lunged, brown legs thrashing out, black heads bobbing. Rajiv was the champion. Once he got the ball it was magic. No one else could get it, he twisted and turned and writhed swifter than a snake . . . like this . . . and like this . . . and like this . . . as he tossed the ball from heel to ankle to knee to toe . . . and passed it across to his team mate and dribbled it back towards the goal post, then wham! A flying kick as he aimed it right through to score a goal!

Suddenly a voice was calling. 'Rajiv! Rajiv!' A figure emerged out of the heat haze, running towards them. It hurt Ben's eyes to look, the light was so bright, but it was her – Sumi! Now he saw her more clearly; saw her laughing face and her shining black plaits flying out behind her just as they always did. Yet she looked different. No longer a child. She wasn't wearing her grey school skirt which Ben was used to seeing, instead she wore a glittering pink saree shot through with silver and green threads which sparkled as she ran, and bangles which jingled on her arms, and earrings which glinted in her ears.

Rajiv dropped the ball and turned towards his sister. He too began to run towards her, but at that moment Ben saw what no one else seemed to see. It was the white Rolls Royce. There it was, gliding across the common. Ben looked in horror. As it passed the old men smoking their hookahs, they disappeared. Now it was driving right up the middle of the common towards the footballers. One by one, they too disappeared and behind was nothing but a black void. Then the car was driving towards Rajiv and Sumi who were still running towards each other. It was going to drive right between them and separate them before they reached each other.

Ben screamed out a warning, but neither Rajiv nor Sumi seemed to hear or see. He began to run. As he ran, he could hear the drumming in his ears. It was getting louder and faster. He ran so fast that he knew he would reach Rajiv before the Rolls Royce. He turned to face the car, his arms spread out protectively, just as the glittering flat, silver grid, with the silver lady on top reaching out for him, came bearing down tipping him into darkness.

Before he fell, he caught a glimpse of Rajiv and Sumi. As they met, she clasped him round his waist and whirled him round and round and round. He could hear their voices shouting and laughing with joy. Then all was black and silent.

Ben's eyes were tightly shut. He wondered if they had been shut all along. He didn't open them but lay listening. He could hear the drum beating once more. It beat softly and steadily.

But now he heard something else. It was the sound of car wheels crunching on the gravel outside. There was the slam of doors, footsteps and voices.

Ben sat up, his eyes wide open. There was Rajiv standing like a statue in the corner of his bedroom on one leg with his arms outstretched. But who was drumming? He turned to where he had been sitting on the floor in the middle of the room.

'Gary!'

'I heard the drumming from the top of the drive, I had to come and see,' said Gary.

Feet were pounding up the stairs and coming towards the bedroom. 'The white Rolls Royce!' gasped Ben. 'It's here!'

At that moment, the bedroom door burst open, and a man and woman stood there with angry faces.

'Rajiv!' exclaimed a loud voice. 'Who are these people?'

Rajiv, the statue, came alive. His eyes opened and they were sharp and clear. He walked towards his aunt and uncle.

'Who gave you permission to have these people in your room?' asked his aunt.

Rajiv came and stood between Ben and Gary. 'They are my friends,' he said firmly. 'Now that you have taken my sister away from me, you must allow me my friends.'

'That is true,' said a soft old voice, and

Grandfather came into the room. 'Go out now, boys, you too, Rajiv. Go out into the sunny afternoon. Here, take your football, and play!'

He picked up Ben's football and handed it to him. 'Go now,' he whispered to Gary. 'You know that Sumi is well and happy. You saw her too, yes?'

Gary nodded. 'Yes, I'm glad,' he said sadly.

Down in the park, the boys were choosing teams. When they saw Gary and Ben, they shouted enthusiastically. 'Come and play! Be on our team!' they vied with each other. No one asked Rajiv.

'I'll come on your team,' Ben told Stephen. 'But only if you'll have Rajiv too!'

'You must be joking,' hissed Stephen angrily. 'You know he's no good. Look what happened last time! Come off it!'

'He's good, I tell you. Have him and I'll come too!' insisted Ben.

'If they have Rajiv, we'd better watch out,' said Gary.

Everyone looked at Gary open-mouthed. Well, if Gary said so . . . perhaps . . .

The game started. The ball went into play. At first tentatively, it was kicked in this direction and in that and off-side, and outside the goal posts. But gradually, as though somewhere a drum began to beat, the ball moved like magic. Rajiv got it between his feet and ran, kicking it this way and that way, from heel to toe to knee to head; passing it from one player to another, then taking possession again and heading it straight for the goal posts. A kick, another kick and an aim, and the ball slammed through into the goal.

The players cheered and shouted! 'Well done, Rajiv!'

A white Rolls Royce came driving slowly by. It stopped and for a while, the occupants stared out at the football players. Then the door opened and Rajiv's grandfather got out. The Rolls Royce drove away and the old man walked towards the game, his face alight with smiles. He had a letter in his hand. Rajiv's parents were coming to see him. As he watched Rajiv in full play, he knew that Lord Shiva danced and all was right with the world.

3
Dawlish Dobson

They met him the day they moved into Lily Cottage. He hung about like a stray dog, nosing his way into everything with the kind of expression which said, 'Don't kick me, I only want to be friendly.'

Edward hated him on sight. Probably because his mother seemed to fall for him hook, line and sinker. The boy was all over her: 'Can I move this in for you, Mrs Thomas? Shall I carry that for you, Mrs Thomas? I'll do that, just leave it to me, Mrs Thomas.' It was enough to make anyone sick, but unbelievably to Edward, his mother just lapped it up, and his dad too. 'What a lovely boy,' they cooed. 'So well behaved! Don't know how some mothers do it. I never could,' and she threw him a reproachful glance.

Edward was furious and stormed upstairs to his new bedroom. He was going to hate it here, he knew it. Moving out to the country! What a stupid idea! Suddenly, overcome with regrets, he sat on the edge of the bed staring at his old football posters through blurred eyes.

His mates in London would all be out in the park playing football and conkering. It was autumn and the horse chestnut trees were laden with conkers. He had been conker champion among his friends; he wondered how he would do here.

'I'd like to get a conker on the end of a string with that twerp – Dawlish – did he say his name was? What kind of a dumb name is that?' he muttered to himself.

His sister came up and stood in the doorway. 'Trust you to pick the best room in the house,' she said peevishly.

'Well, I bagged it first,' retorted Edward defensively. 'So what?'

'Only because you pushed your way in front like a big bully,' she complained.

'Oh, shut up, Marie,' he said roughly.

'What's going on?' Her twin sister Lisa peered over her shoulder. 'Got the best room in the house, I see,' she exclaimed. 'How does he do it!'

'Muscle!' said Marie, clenching her fist.

Edward bared his teeth at them and held up a comic as if to hurl it at them.

'O.K. O.K.' They giggled, and everyone relaxed.

'Has he gone yet?' asked Edward.

'Who?' asked his sisters.

'That twit, Dawlish – what a stupid name! Has he gone?'

'No! Mum's just giving him a drink. She said to come down if you wanted one too.'

'No, I don't!' snarled Edward resentfully. 'Not while he's here, at any rate.'

The twins giggled. 'Don't you like him, Edward?' they chimed.

'He's wet,' muttered Edward.

Later when he finally went down, drawn by the smell of cooking, Dawlish had gone, and he found his mum and dad getting a meal together in the kitchen.

'Oh there you are, Edward!' cried his mother. 'Help your dad unpack some plates and cutlery. They should all be in that crate over there.' She indicated a packing crate which Dad was levering open.

'Come on, Edward. Don't just stand there!' said Dad impatiently. 'Here, get these on the table.'

Edward took the plates and knives and forks as they were unearthed, and put them on the table. He was starving, and glad that his mother immediately began to serve a steaming hot stew. But they had only just sat down and barely eaten a mouthful, when there was a knock on the door.

'Who's that?' They all looked up wonderingly. Dad answered the door.

Three girls clustered on the doorstep. They giggled and shuffled uncertainly, as if they had dared themselves to knock, and each nudged the other to speak up for them all. At last one girl, blushing furiously, said, 'Do you need any help moving in?' They peered past Mr Thomas, sizing up the family. Their eyes rested mockingly for a moment on Edward, then moved on to the twins. They seemed to be of an age with them – about ten years old. 'We can show you things,' they said. 'Like the well. You have a well in your garden, you know!'

'Oh really!' exclaimed Mr Thomas. 'That's very interesting. We'd be very pleased for you to show us things, but can you come back later? As you can see, we're just about to eat.'

The girls nodded vigorously, then turned and ran giggling down the path.

After they had eaten, and when everyone had helped to wash up and do some more unpacking, Mum said the children could go out and explore a little.

Lisa and Marie were quick off the mark and were out of the door and down the path before you could say 'Jack Robinson'.

Edward had hesitated, and his dad called, 'Hey, Edward! Before you go, give us a hand shifting this chest.'

Edward pulled a face. 'Can't I do it later, Dad . . . I . . .'

Suddenly, there was Dawlish lounging in the doorway. 'I'll give you a hand, Mr Thomas,' he said with a broad smile.

'Thanks, Dawlish,' exclaimed Mr Thomas with a sideways glance at Edward. 'Many hands make light work!' and they all heaved.

Of course, after that, Dawlish stayed on chatting, and Mum offered him another drink and Dad questioned him about the neighbourhood. Dawlish seemed a mine of information. He told them about Mr Munday across the road, who was a master carpenter, and still capable of hammering a nail or two although he was ninety-one; and there was Mr Reeks, the blacksmith. 'Used to shoe horses, but now makes metal gates and railings.' Then he told them about Elsie Dean, who knew everything there is to know about herbs. 'There's people round these parts who've never been to a doctor in their lives. They prefer Elsie. My dad's like that,' said Dawlish.

'Oh!' exclaimed Mrs Thomas, interrupting. It was the first time that Dawlish had mentioned any family. 'And what does your dad do?'

To their surprise, Dawlish suddenly looked uncomfortable and his cheeks flushed slightly. 'He's er . . . in business. Yes, that's it, he's a business man!' He recovered himself rapidly. 'Well, I'd best be off now!' and to Edward's amazement, Dawlish had gone, just when he feared he would be stuck with him for the afternoon.

Edward wandered slowly down to the gate. He peered furtively up and down the lane, but it was deserted. There was no sign of the girls, and he wondered what they were up to. He wished enviously that he was as good at making friends as Lisa and Marie.

Suddenly there was a whirr of bicycles. They seemed to come out of nowhere. A bunch of boys whooshed by, and all, it seemed, turned their heads simultaneously and stared at him as they passed. Then they were gone. Round the bend and out of sight.

Edward raced back to the cottage shouting, 'Mum? I'm just going out on my bike!'

The bicycles had been the last things to be unloaded from the removal van, so they were right there leaning up against the shed. With a tremor of excitement, Edward pushed his bike down into the lane and cycled off in the direction of the others.

The road stretched ahead of him straight and clear and visible all the way out of the village. But there was no sign of the boys. He paused for a moment, puzzled and uncertain whether to carry on. Then he noticed a track leading off to the left. It was a dirt track, but well-worn, so Edward decided to follow it. For a while, the track ran between a cluster of higgledy-piggledy cottages, none of them very well cared for, with bumpy roofs and tumbling down walls, and rabbit hutches peeking out of overgrown gardens. Then unexpectedly, the village was left behind, and the track was running across rough land skirting the edge of a long line of woods which rose steeply above the houses. The track, however, was still good, and the cycling easy, so Edward carried on, feeling the thrill of exploration and proud of his confidence and bravery in pushing on into the unknown.

Suddenly, he heard a ferocious growl, and before Edward could take any action, a huge dog shot out of the woods towards him. He could see his bared teeth, sharp as knives, dangerous as a shark's jaw. There was no point in trying to cycle away, Edward knew the dog could easily catch up with him. So he stopped and desperately put out a hand calling, 'Good boy! Down, boy!' But the dog circled him snarling and snapping and began to leap at his jacket, nipping at his cuffs. As Edward tried to back off, he lost his balance, and he and the bike tumbled into a heap with the dog now leaping across his chest. Edward felt the hot breath in his face, then he heard a commanding bellow, almost as ferocious as the dog's barks. 'Get off him, you hell hound. Go on! Off!' A large, black-bearded, rough-looking man wearing trousers held up by a thick leather buckled belt, and stumpy, well-worn boots, came striding out of the woods holding a wooden staff, taller than himself.

The dog fell back, his tail suddenly curling down between his legs, and he cringed as the man approached prodding at him with his stick. He swore at the animal as he bent down and clipped a lead to the choker round its neck, then with a mighty yank so that the dog whimpered, he strode off without so much as looking at Edward to see if he was all right.

Edward lay rigid in a state of shock, not daring to move until the man and his dog had receded down the track and out of sight. Then stiffly, he tried to extricate himself from his bicycle.

'You O.K.?' He felt the weight of the bike lifted from his body, and he found himself looking up into the face of Dawlish Dobson, his thin, languid body drooped over him, concerned, and his eyes darted round, afraid.

Edward struggled to his feet and took his bicycle from Dawlish. His heart was thudding furiously and he wanted to cry.

'I'll walk back home with you,' offered Dawlish.

'No!' Edward exploded roughly. 'No. Thanks. I'll be O.K.' and he flipped his bike round in the direction of the village and pedalled off home.

The next day was school. The twins were thrilled and didn't seem to care that they were going in mid-term. Everything was new, and they loved it; new home, new school, new friends, new school uniform! They scampered around like excited squirrels hunting for blouses, knickers, socks and shoes; squabbling about pencils and satchels and notebooks, and gobbling down their breakfasts so fast that Mum had to shout, 'Stop! You'll be sick!'

Edward felt sick. He got dressed in slow motion and had to be persuaded and cajoled every bit of the way. It was all right for Lisa and Marie. They had friends already. He was going to have to walk through a classroom door and be the only new boy in the class. Everyone would stare at him. Everyone would have their own friends and their own groups. Who would like him? Perhaps they would tease him about his sticky-out ears; perhaps they would joke about the way he spoke. Perhaps they would knock him around in the playground or trip him up. At his other school, he had been considered rather good at football, and he had many friends. Would they think so here? What a dumb, stupid thing it was to move, he thought miserably.

Mrs Thomas walked them all to school. It was a long walk, right through the village, on and on until the road turned steeply and climbed the hill past the church. The walk turned into a procession, as more and more children joined them. Edward felt conspicuous. No one else had their mothers or fathers along.

'Mum! Must you come any further? We'll be O.K,' he pleaded.

'Don't be ridiculous, Edward,' said his mother firmly. 'I've got to see you and the twins into school on your first day.'

Then Lisa and Marie saw their new friends Chloë and Michelle and rushed ahead to catch up with them, and Edward was left walking alone beside his mother. He felt like a baby. He felt humiliated. He was sure people were noticing and staring at him. He dropped behind hoping no one would realise they were together. This hope was shattered by a loud shout. 'Hey! Mrs Thomas! Hello, Edward!' It was Dawlish who rushed upon them like long-lost friends and always with that same sweet smile on his face which made Edward feel sick.

Of course Mrs Thomas gushed all over him. 'Oh, Dawlish, how good to see you. Edward needs someone that he knows to go into school with. I hope you'll keep an eye on him for me.'

'Course I will,' cried Dawlish, grinning at Edward who was so embarrassed he wanted the ground to open and swallow him up.

They reached the school gates. Edward viewed them with his heart in his boots. Only the sight of the two solitary goal posts, standing like sculptures on the broad, open space of the playing field, lifted his spirits just a little.

Yet, the first day at school was not at all what Edward expected. It was terrible, of course, but not in the way he had imagined. Yes, everyone did stare at him when he walked in through the classroom door; yes, they did poke fun at his accent and the way he spoke; yes, sure enough, someone did call him 'Big Ears', but the biggest surprise was the way in which they treated Dawlish. When the teacher said, 'Edward, would you like to sit next to Dawlish as you seem to be friends already,' everyone sniggered and someone held his nose.

'Stop it, now!' exclaimed the teacher angrily. 'Edward! Sit over there between Carol and Dawlish, and don't let's have any more nonsense from the rest of you.'

As the day went on, Edward noticed that it was Dawlish they tried to trip up; Dawlish who they picked fights with in the playground; Dawlish who they chanted names at, like 'Jippy, Jippy! Dirty Gipsy!'

'He's a gipsy,' Carol informed him.

'So what?' asked Edward.

'Do you know why they called him Dawlish?' she went on. 'Because he was born in Dawlish! You know, the seaside town in Devon. Fancy being named after a seaside town! Stupid, isn't it? They travel around, you see. Don't live in proper houses like us, so my dad says, "you never know where they've been!"' and she laughed at the joke.

At breaktime, some boys rushed up to Edward and asked him if he'd like to play marbles with them.

'Oh yes!' cried Edward feeling pleased. He had brought some of his marbles with him and fumbled to get them out of his pocket. But as he bent down to play in a corner of the playground, he looked up and saw Dawlish. He was standing by himself. No one had asked him to play. He stood watching and solemn. 'How strange,' thought Edward to himself. 'That's how I thought it would be for me,' and with a slight twinge of guilt, he tossed his first marble.

At lunch time, Dawlish tried to sit next to Edward, but someone pushed him roughly aside and took the place instead; and after school, Dawlish hung around waiting for Edward to get his anorak. He seemed to want to show the other children that Edward was his friend. But though there were cries of 'Bye, Edward! See you tomorrow!', no one said 'goodbye' to Dawlish.

Edward didn't want to be seen walking out of school with Dawlish, and he hated it when he saw his mother waiting at the gates for them. 'Hello, Edward! Hello, Dawlish! Did you have a good day today?'

A group of children hanging on the railings nearby sniggered and mimicked her quietly. But Edward heard and blushed to his roots.

The twins came barging up all full of themselves, their voices lapping and over-lapping as they told their mother about their day. Edward wondered if Dawlish would now leave them and go home, but he didn't. Instead he stayed close by and set off walking down the hill with them, glancing over his shoulder from time to time as if checking his safety. Edward noticed a gang of bigger boys who seemed to be trailing along some distance behind them until they reached the centre of the village, then they dispersed and had completely disappeared by the time they reached Lily Cottage. 'Now, will he go?' thought Edward. But when Dawlish said, 'Well I'd better be off then,' he made no move to be off, but looked longingly up the garden path to the kitchen door like a dog looking for scraps.

'Can you stop for a drink and a biscuit?' asked Mrs Thomas kindly.

Edward gave a furious sigh. Need she ask!

'You want to watch that boy,' a neighbour advised Mrs Thomas a week or so later when it was noticed how much Dawlish was round their house. 'Gipsies, you know. You never can tell. His mum and dad are out on the road at this moment. They leave the boy with his grandfather. It gives him a bit of a chance to go to school. 'Course, he can hardly read nor write, but they'll be round soon enough to take him away, and then we won't see nothing of them for a year maybe.'

'Oh dear!' sighed Mrs Thomas sympathetically.

'He's just trying to be part of our family,' hissed Edward to his sisters. No matter how much he ignored Dawlish at school, he was round their house afterwards almost every day for his drink and biscuit. Mum was soft-hearted and explained it was because he probably wasn't getting much mothering what with his parents being away, and living with an old grandad whom everyone said was very fierce.

Then one day at school, the children decided to play a game called 'Chicken Run'. Edward had never played it before. The children stood in two lines making a kind of corridor. Then someone was chosen to try and run down the corridor and get to the end without being stopped. They could grab at you, tug your arms and try and trip you up, and the person would jump and wriggle and pull away, while everyone would chant, 'chicken, chicken, chicken,' until they made it to the end. It was fun. Everyone joined in, except Dawlish. He crept off into the toilets and stayed there until the end of break.

But after school, the children took it out on Dawlish. 'Too chicken to play, were you?' they taunted. 'Well, it's your turn now!' Dawlish made a dash for the cloakrooms. A group of children followed in hot pursuit. They would have caught him but for the fact they ran straight into a teacher.

'Children!' he bellowed. 'How many times have you been told to walk not run. Get back to where you started from and begin again, properly.'

Edward went to the cloakroom, but Dawlish had already gone. Then he heard distant chanting coming from outside. He couldn't help feeling uneasy as he hurried out of school. 'Chicken, chicken, chicken,' they shouted.

Two lines had formed on either side of the gates, and wavering this way and that, wondering whether he dared run through, was Dawlish. Every now and then he made a run at the corridor, but he only got a few paces in before rough hands grabbed him and feet tripped him up. He managed to shake himself loose and retreated out of reach, hovering uncertainly like an animal at bay.

Then suddenly, he turned and ran to the other side of the playground. He had the element of surprise, and before anyone could move, he had flung himself over the wall and was soon a speck in the distance.

'Oh!' There were groans of disappointment. 'Never mind, we'll get him next time,' cried a voice.

Edward found the twins waiting for him. 'What did they want to do to Dawlish?' they asked.

'Oh nothing! It's just a game called "Chicken",' murmured Edward casually. 'Just a bit of fun.'

'Dawlish looked scared,' said Lisa.

"Course not. It's nothing. They did it to me too,' boasted Edward.

'Hello! Beat you home!' called out a cheery voice as they walked in through the kitchen door. It was Dawlish, beaming away at them, sitting all nicely at home in front of a drink and biscuits.

'He's been fetching coal in for me,' smiled Mrs Thomas, 'so I gave him his drink straight away.' She kissed her children, but Edward pulled back, jealousy rushing up in his throat. 'I'm going upstairs,' he said gruffly.

Up in his room, he thrust his hands in his anorak to get out his marbles, but his fingers felt nothing. With panic mounting, he felt in this pocket, then that; his trouser pockets and back again to his anorak pockets, but they were gone.

Edward rushed downstairs. 'My marbles! They've gone!' he shouted. 'I had them at school, in the playground, but now they've gone. They were in my anorak pocket!'

He stopped short and looked hard at Dawlish. Dawlish had been in the cloakroom almost alone. People said gipsies were thieves. Thief, thief, thief! The word pounded in his brain. His voice didn't say it, but his eyes did.

Dawlish looked at him and blushed. Then he got to his feet and said, 'Well, I'd best be going now. Thanks ever so much for the drink and biscuits, Mrs Thomas,' and he let himself out. The Thomas family looked at each other. 'You don't think . . .' whispered one of the twins.

'Of course not,' said Mum, looking upset. 'Dawlish is our friend. He's been like one of the family. Oh dear, I hope he didn't think we were accusing him.'

'Well, he could have!' muttered Edward stubbornly. 'I know they were in my anorak pocket, and my anorak was in the cloakroom, and Dawlish was there before I was. He could have.'

'Edward,' said Mrs Thomas sternly. 'Anyone could have. Without real evidence, to even think someone is a thief is bad. If they're lost they're lost. I'm sorry, but please don't go suspecting everyone and anyone.'

Edward stumped back upstairs. He was sure his marbles had been stolen, and he was sure it was Dawlish.

Word got round school that Edward's marbles were missing, and all the children looked at Dawlish. There was a kind of buzz in the air, and somehow, Edward felt it had made him even more popular. He had given them a reason to torment Dawlish, and now they were going to use it. There were gleeful whispers behind hands and in corners of the playground, 'Chicken run, chicken run, chicken run! This time, we'll get him.'

The school bell rang. There was a rush for the cloakroom. Several children got sent back to class for running and had to set out again, but others got there in time. This time, Dawlish hung back.

'Come along, Dawlish,' said a teacher impatiently. 'Get on home with you, I want my tea!'

Edward had lingered to watch out for Dawlish. As he passed Dawlish, he whispered, 'I never took your marbles.'

It started as something small. The teachers knew the game and smiled. It was just a bit of fun. No one ever got hurt. First there was a small chicken run in the cloakrooms. Dawlish grabbed his jacket, then ducked and tugged and wriggled and ran out into the playground. But there at the gates was another corridor, this time made by the bigger boys.

Dawlish stood transfixed as if turned to stone. His eyes darted about. Which way could he go? He knew he couldn't make it through the chicken run at the gate. They were beginning to chant, 'Chicken, chicken, chicken!' He looked once more at the wall. It was his only chance. He turned and ran, and with a desperate leap, hurled himself over the wall. But this time, they were waiting for him; they had remembered from last time. Feet kicked and tripped, fingers clawed and tore at him, voices hissed in his ear. Somehow, he wriggled and ducked and kicked and struggled, and suddenly he rolled free and was up on his feet and away.

There were cries of, 'He's getting away! Quick!' Then everyone was running. 'Come on!' Someone grabbed Edward's sleeve. 'Come on! This is great!' Then he was running too. They ran across the playing fields, over the wall on the other side, into the nearby newly ploughed furrows of a farmer's field, they ran, their feet getting heavier from the soft, red soil which clung to their shoes; on and on they ran into the woods – and then they saw him. 'Chicken, chicken, chicken,' they chanted. Edward chanted too.

Dawlish was loping clumsily ahead. He was tired now, and clutching his side as though he had a stitch. The children sensed they could reach their target and shouted even louder as they charged nearer. An old caravan parked in a muddy clearing came into view. Dawlish stumbled over a lumpy root which had straggled across the track, and with a wild cry fell in a painful heap.

The children gave a whoop of triumph. They rushed forward to encircle him. At that moment, the caravan door flew open, and there stood the huge, black-bearded man, with staff in hand and the dog on its leash. He gave a roar of rage and let loose the dog. The children fled, their screams scattering through the woods in all directions.

The dog was bounding and barking straight towards Dawlish. Edward looked in horror. He saw the dog's bared teeth and heard its fearsome growls. Dawlish would be killed. He grabbed a fallen branch from the ground and rushed forward to protect the boy yelling like a savage, 'Go away! Go away!' and he waved the leafy branch before him.

The dog kept coming, and suddenly was all over Dawlish. Edward was sure he would be ripped to pieces, when, to his amazement, he was up on his knees and had flung his arms around the dog's neck. 'Good boy, good boy,' he wept, and the dog licked his face and wagged his tail for all it was worth.

The big man with the stick was advancing menacingly. 'Clear off!' he bellowed at Edward. 'You young savages! How dare you attack my grandson.'

Edward flung down the branch, and ran as if he had wings on his heels.

There were solemn faces in the kitchen when he got home. He looked at his father and mother and the twins, who stared up at him with large, worried eyes.

'What's up?' he asked, panting and gasping. 'I'm sorry I'm late . . . I . . .'

'We know what's happened,' said Mrs

Thomas, and her eyes fell on an anorak slung over a chair.

'My anorak!' gasped Edward. Then stopped short. It couldn't be. He was wearing it.

'Take that off and put this on,' ordered Mr Thomas.

Silently, Edward did as his father told him.

'Now put your hand in your pocket.'

Edward did. His fingers closed over four, cool, hard marbles. His marbles.

'You took the wrong anorak by mistake,' said his mother gently.

Edward burst into tears.

The next day, Dawlish wasn't in school. Straight after school was over, Edward slipped away into the woods. All he knew was that he wanted to say 'sorry', and he wanted to present Dawlish with his four marbles.

He didn't run, but walked slowly over the furrowed field into the wood. It had been autumn when they arrived in the village and there had been a blaze of sunny days. But now, today, he realised that most of the leaves had dulled and dropped; the colours had faded into the greys and browns of winter.

He followed the track along until he came to the clearing. It was empty. The caravan had gone. There were deep ruts in the ground where it had stood, and tyre marks in the mud where a car had come and towed it away.

Dawlish Dobson had gone.

4

My Name is Jasmine Grey

The girl stood in the doorway. A light came from somewhere, a bit of thin afternoon sun, and caught her tight, burnished afro curls and seemed to set them on fire.

'Hello, Jasmine.' It was Bob who spoke first. Then he turned encouragingly and looked at his wife, Lena.

'Hello, Jasmine,' said Lena. She stepped forward shyly, not wishing to seem too eager.

'Well, it's good to meet you at last!' said Bob brightly, but immediately felt foolish.

Jasmine stood stiffly in the doorway with her eyes down. Then Aunty Sheila, who ran the Children's Home, came bustling through to break the ice. 'Jasmine,' she cried, putting a loose arm around the girl and urging her into the room. 'This is Mr and Mrs Jacobs who have been making enquiries about you after they saw your picture in the paper.'

Lena glanced at a newspaper cutting in her

hand then looked up at the girl.

'You're much prettier in real life,' she smiled.

'Yeh!' agreed Bob warmly.

It had been Bob's idea to adopt. He and Lena had been trying to have their own child ever since they married five years ago, but none had come along.

'I can't see anything wrong with either of you,' the doctor told them. 'I suggest you relax and forget about the whole thing, and before you know it you'll have a baby on the way.'

But Bob had been adopted himself and he suggested they adopt a child too. 'We can give a child a home, and then if we do have a baby of our own, we'll be bringing it into a ready-made family.'

Lena, though, had been a bit doubtful. 'I don't know if I can love a child which isn't our own,' she murmured.

'Of course you can!' exclaimed Bob confidently. 'I know you. You are such a loving person. You love everything that breathes. Stray kittens, lost dogs – and look how you love your sister's children, and look how they love you. You're a perfect mother and the perfect adoptive mother,' Bob kissed her reassuringly, 'and I should know!'

So they had made enquiries and waited patiently to find the right child.

Then one day, Lena showed Bob an advertisement in the paper. It was under the heading, 'Fostering and Adoption'. There was a rather blurred photograph of a girl of about nine years old. She stared out at them solemnly as if she didn't believe anyone could love her. Underneath her picture, they printed her own description of herself. 'My name is Jasmine Grey. I am nine years old. I like listening to reggae music. I like dogs and I like roller-skating. I am half Afro-Carribean and half-white, so I would like to find a mixed-race family.'

'That's us!' said Bob. 'Shall we make enquiries?'

'Yes!' breathed Lena slowly, her eyes fixed on the picture. 'Yes, let's try and see her.'

They wrote letters, made telephone calls and had lots of interviews with people wanting to know if Lena and Bob would make good parents, then at last, a meeting with Jasmine was arranged; just a short meeting, at the children's home, to see whether or not they liked each other and to see if they wanted to get to know each other better.

The three of them stared at each other. Thoughts and questions raced through their heads. The Jacobs looked at Jasmine and thought, 'Will she become our own little girl? Could we love her? Will she love us? Will she want to live with us?' And Jasmine thought . . . well, who knows what Jasmine thought? Perhaps it was more feelings. She knew she wanted to belong to a family . . .

but . . . there, her thoughts stopped.

Aunty Sheila said, 'Jasmine dear, go and fetch your photograph album. I'm sure Mr and Mrs Jacobs would be very interested to see how you've grown up.'

Without a word, Jasmine turned and disappeared. 'She'll be a bit reserved at first. She's already had one or two tries at being adopted, and it hasn't worked out. They don't always, you know, and it's best to be truthful and acknowledge it. It's hard to really love, you know.'

'Yeh!' said Bob, with feeling. 'It brings it all back. I can remember when I was being adopted too.'

Jasmine returned, clutching the photograph album. Bob and Lena had sat down on the settee, and they made a space for her between them. But Jasmine just laid down the album in the empty space and removed herself to a chair at the far end of the room.

There weren't many photographs. Perhaps one page for every year of her life. They showed her growing up from babyhood, through being a toddler in the children's home nursery, a young child digging with a bucket and spade on some seashore, to a neat schoolgirl refusing to smile for the photographer as she posed in her grey and maroon school uniform.

'We brought one or two photos, too,' said

Lena, fumbling in her bag. 'Here's one of our house. This is our garden – we've got a swing in it, and this is Bramble, our dog.'

'Oh!' The sound of interest which escaped Jasmine's lips startled them all. 'I didn't know you had a dog,' she said.

'Yes, look!' Lena held the photograph closer for Jasmine to see.

Jasmine looked, just long enough, but then sank back in her chair once more with her eyes down.

'Would you like to come and see Bramble? He loves children,' asked Bob. But Jasmine didn't reply, and spoke no more that day.

Later, after they had had a cup of tea, Aunty Sheila showed them to the door. There were tears in Lena's eyes. 'She doesn't like us, does she?'

'Be patient. Don't give up easily. Come again next week.'

'We won't give up yet,' said Bob, squeezing his wife's arm. 'You didn't expect her to throw herself at us, did you? No, I know what it was like. I can remember. You're scared. Jasmine's scared. Scared we won't like her or that she won't like us. Of course we'll be patient and see what happens.'

That night, when Aunty Sheila sat by Jasmine's bed to tell her a bedtime story, she said, 'If you want, you can see the Jacobs next week, would you like that?'

'Perhaps,' murmured Jasmine. 'If they bring Bramble.'

On their next visit, the Jacobs brought Bramble with them.

Lena wasn't sure if they had done the right thing. But Jasmine was thrilled to bits. She turned into a normal little girl, chatting excitably, hugging and laughing with the dog – but only with the dog. If either Lena or Bob tried to talk to her, she ignored them or looked the other way.

When they were leaving, she asked when they would come again.

Lena said later, 'It's only because of the dog.'

But the visits continued even though Jasmine's main interest still seemed to be only with Bramble. Gradually, the Jacobs got to know her. They found out that although she said her favourite food was sausages, chips and beans, she loved the really hot spicy curries which Lena was so good at cooking. And as for her love of *pappadums*, Bob said she should go into the *Guinness Book of Records* for eating a whole packet of *pappadums* which Lena had deep-fried one day. Fourteen, to be exact!

Now Jasmine was going to the Jacobs' house for weekends. They had prepared a bedroom specially for her, painting the walls creamy white, with yellow, pink and green flowery curtains and bedspread to match. The only trouble was, although Bob tucked her up and read her a bedtime story till she fell asleep, they never found her in her bed the next morning. Some time in the night, Jasmine always found her way down to the dog basket and slept there. Bramble, it seemed, heroically and uncomplainingly, made way for her, and removed himself to the rug in front of the fireplace.

So the months passed by and the summer holidays came round. Lena and Bob invited Jasmine to come and stay for as long as she liked. They promised her trips to the seaside and perhaps one to Rainbow Land Funfair where she could spend the day going on all the rides. Jasmine listened with her eyes cast down and nothing on her face to tell them what she thought of the idea. Finally she had said, 'I'll come if Bramble will be there.'

'We can't adopt her just because she loves Bramble,' cried Lena in despair. 'Doesn't she care anything for us?'

Aunt Sheila said, 'Let's see how you all get on in the holidays and then you can decide.'

Jasmine sat on the seesaw trying to bounce it up and down on her own. She felt lonely. Bob and Lena lived just too far away for her to see her usual friends. Anyway, most of them were away. She had wanted to bring Bramble down to the swings too, but Lena said he would be too much for her to control on her own, so now she sat alone feeling surly and sorry for herself.

Two other girls had come along and were messing around on the swings laughing and joking, but neither of them even looked at her. 'Lena's mean,' Jasmine thought angrily to herself, wanting someone to blame for her loneliness. But she knew she was being unfair. Lena had tried to introduce her to other children of her age in the neighbourhood, but Jasmine had rejected them, making Lena feel that the more she did to try to make her feel wanted, the more Jasmine pushed her away.

Jasmine scowled into the distance. Then she saw a small speck of a person running, running across the wide expanse of green playing field. It was a girl, with ponytail flying and feet that hardly seemed to touch the ground as she raced alongside a floppy-eared cocker spaniel on the end of a lead. 'If she's allowed to take the dog out, why can't I?' was Jasmine's first thought.

The girl reached the swings, calling out to the other two girls as she bent down and tied the dog up to one of the poles.

'Hi, Tracey! Hi, Melanie!'

'Give us a push, Rachel!' the girls called back.

Rachel did, grabbing the seat of first one and then the other, running forwards and back until she thrust each up as high as she could.

'Right! I'm having a go on the seesaw now,'

she called out. She turned round, and without so much as a by your leave, heaved down the other end of the seesaw, tipping Jasmine up into the air. She leapt astride and the two girls balanced almost evenly in the middle, their toes lightly touching the ground as they stared into each other's faces for the first time. Then Rachel bounced heavily, bringing herself lower so that she could push the ground hard with her feet, sending herself up into the air.

For a while, and without a word being exchanged, the two of them seesawed vigorously. As the seesaw bumped down on the ground, whoever was in the air nearly flew off, and both girls began to laugh and squeal with the enjoyment of it.

'What's your dog's name?' shouted Jasmine.

'Polly!' answered Rachel.

'I've got a dog too. His name's Bramble,' boasted Jasmine.

'What sort?' asked Rachel.

'Oh . . . er . . .' Jasmine felt stupid and caught out. She didn't know what kind of dog Bramble was. 'A sort of mixture,' she stumbled lamely. 'Can we walk him? Your dog, I mean?' she asked.

'It's a she – Polly,' corrected Rachel. She slowed the seesaw down. 'Yes, if you like.'

'We're off to walk Polly down by the stream. You coming too?' Rachel called to the other girls.

But Melanie and Tracey were swinging away. 'No! We like swinging!' they shouted. 'See you!'

The two girls slid off the seesaw. Jasmine rushed over to the tethered dog and knelt down to give her a hug. 'Oh you lovely boy,' she murmured writhing under her excitable licking. 'Where shall we take him?'

'HER!' cried Rachel emphatically. 'Polly's a girl.'

'Oh sorry,' muttered Jasmine. 'I always think of dogs as he and cats as she. Silly.'

'Let's go down to the stream,' suggested Rachel. 'Polly loves water and she gets a drink too.'

The stream ran along the fence which divided a newly built housing estate from the park.

'I just live over there, see!' Rachel pointed to a house with a cherry tree growing in the garden. 'We haven't been here very long. I start at the comprehensive next term.'

'We live in an old house,' said Jasmine. 'It's by the front gate of the park. Perhaps I'll go to your school.'

'Oh yeh! We could go together,' exclaimed Rachel enthusiastically.

Rachel let Polly off the lead and they all dashed into the water. It was very shallow, and hardly covered their shins, but they splashed about and slapped water at each other until they were wet through.

Finally they came out and threw themselves down on the grassy bank to dry out. As they lay side by side, Rachel lifted up one white arm to the sky. Jasmine raised one black arm to compare.

'I'd like to get a nice tan,' murmured Rachel, 'but not as much as you!' She laughed.

'You just haven't been cooked enough,' joked Jasmine. 'They took you out of the oven too soon.'

'But they left you in too long, and you burnt, didn't you?' Rachel quipped back, and prodded her till she rolled around giggling.

'You know what, though,' cried Rachel suddenly sitting up and staring hard at Jasmine. 'I wish I could frizz my hair up like yours.'

'That's easy,' said Jasmine. 'Just plait it. Look, I'll do it now for you, if you like.'

Rachel immediately pulled out her ponytail and shook her hair loose. Jasmine knelt behind her and began to divide it into dozens of small bunches which she then plaited tightly.

The sun was just touching the tops of the houses and sinking fast, when Jasmine finally plaited the last tuft of blonde hair. 'There. Finished,' she said standing up with a look of satisfaction.

Rachel touched her head all over tentatively feeling the dozens of little plaits. 'Feels funny,' she said. 'Let's go to my house. I want to see in the mirror.'

'You look African,' teased Jasmine. 'Just like me!'

'Oh no! What'll my mum say!' Rachel called Polly out of the stream, and she rushed out all dripping wet and shook herself all over them. 'Come on! Let's go.' She put Polly on the lead.

Jasmine noticed the long shadows of the houses falling like witches' hats across the playing fields. 'I think I'd better go home,' she said. 'Lena – er – I mean, my mum will be worried. Sleep in the plaits and don't take them out till tomorrow.'

As they parted, Rachel suddenly turned round and called out, 'Hey! I don't know your name!'

'Jasmine! My name is Jasmine Grey.'

'Bye, Jasmine! See you tomorrow.'

Jasmine went home skipping, but she walked through the front door with a sulky face. 'What's the matter, love?' asked Lena anxiously.

'I've got a friend,' said Jasmine with a frown.

'Oh that's wonderful!' exclaimed Lena giving her a hug. But when she felt her stiff body, and saw her gloomy face, she added, 'Isn't it?'

'You've got a face as long as a bus,' commented Bob with raised eyebrows. 'Why aren't you pleased about it?'

'Because she's allowed to take her dog to the

park but you won't let me,' she pouted. 'Why can't I walk Bramble?'

'You know why, love,' said Bob gently. 'Bramble's a big dog. He's knocked Lena over many a time, and even I can hardly hold him if he puts his mind to it! And he's not that obedient. He doesn't always do as he's told. It would be too risky to let you take him out alone.'

'What kind of dog has your friend got?' asked Lena.

'A cocker spaniel,' muttered Jasmine through clenched teeth.

'What, love? I didn't catch it,' asked Lena who hadn't understood Jasmine's mumble.

'A cocker spaniel,' Jasmine shouted angrily.

'There's no need to shout, dear,' said Lena coolly. 'I didn't hear you the first time. If you think about it carefully, you'll see why we can't let you walk Bramble. He's part Alsatian so he's miles bigger than your friend's cocker spaniel. You can see that. Maybe when you're bigger and Bramble knows you better, maybe then . . .'

'Maybe,' sniffed Jasmine rudely, and flounced upstairs.

Bob and Lena looked at each other sadly and shrugged. 'Poor kid! She's got so much anger inside her. It's going to be difficult,' said Bob giving his wife a squeeze. 'Do you think you can stand it?'

Lena nodded. 'I think so,' she said. 'Any child would feel the same, wouldn't they?'

That night as usual Jasmine didn't sleep in her bed, but neither did she sleep in Bramble's dog basket. Next morning, Lena found her curled up under the dining-room table.

But Jasmine and Rachel did become friends. Rachel and Jasmine. Jasmine and Rachel. Their names became linked as if they were one. Each day Jasmine was either at Rachel's house or Rachel at Jasmine's house. Each day Rachel walked her dog, Polly. Each day Jasmine asked if she could walk Bramble, but the answer was always 'no'. But Rachel often let Jasmine walk Polly on the lead and gradually the summer days passed by and Jasmine seemed to settle down. Gradually she seemed to treat Bob and Lena like her mother and father, and turned their house into her home. They had begun to love seeing her jacket tossed over a chair, or her shoes kicked into the porch. And yet, Jasmine still wouldn't sleep in her bed all night, and they never knew where they would find her when they came downstairs each morning; under the kitchen table, behind the settee, or in the coat cupboard. It was never the same place twice.

One day, Rachel came rushing over to Jasmine flushed with excitement. 'Do you know what?' she squealed. 'Any day now, I'm going to be an aunty!'

'What you?' Jasmine was incredulous. 'You're too young.'

'No, I'm not. It's my sister, see. She's eleven years older than me. I was an accident, see—' She laughed. 'She got married last year. I was a bridesmaid. You ever been a bridesmaid?' She continued as Jasmine solemnly shook her head, 'Ooo, I had such a lovely dress. Anyhow, now she's going to have a baby. My mum's going over to stay with her tomorrow and my gran's coming to look after us.'

'Oh,' said Jasmine. She suddenly felt hollow inside. She would never be an aunt – not a real one. She would never be a bridesmaid.

'Would you like to see my bridesmaid's dress?' asked Rachel brightly.

'O.K.,' said Jasmine, without much enthusiasm.

'We could play dressing up and things. Can you bring something too?'

When Jasmine asked Lena for something to dress up in, Lena found her a beautiful saree with lots of gold and silver threads in it. The next afternoon Jasmine draped it round herself and, very excited, rushed over to Rachel's house.

To her surprise, the front door was shut. Usually when there was someone home, the door was wide open. So Jasmine rang the bell. After a while, the door opened and she found herself looking into the face of a stranger. It

113

was an older woman, with smartly cut dyed blonde hair looking a little too smart for the time of day in her tight black trousers and large gold earrings.

She looked coldly at Jasmine. 'Yes?' she said, without opening the door wider to let her in.

'I've come to play with Rachel. Is she home?' asked Jasmine.

'She's busy,' said the woman. 'I don't think she can play today.'

'Hey, Gran!' Rachel's voice called urgently from upstairs. 'Is that Jasmine? I've been waiting for her. Hey, Jaz! Come on upstairs. I've got a surprise for you.'

So this was Rachel's gran who had come to look after them. Jasmine and she stared silently at each other, then without a word or a smile, the woman opened the door and gestured her in with a toss of her head.

Jasmine slid past and ran upstairs hoisting her saree round her waist. Rachel was in her room and the door was almost closed. 'Wait, wait, wait!' she called. 'Don't come in yet. I'm not quite ready.'

Jasmine stood outside, and took the time to arrange herself. She draped the saree so that it fell round her shoulders and down to the ground in long, flowing pleats. 'You can come in now,' Rachel summoned her.

Jasmine pushed open the door and went inside. There, sitting in the middle of the room looking like a princess, was Rachel. She was wearing her bridesmaid's dress. It was a pale pink with puffed sleeves, a slim bodice round which was tied a broad flowing sash and a skirt which puffed out making her look as if she could float away. And that wasn't all. Round her afro-frizzed head of hair which frothed out like a golden halo, she had bound a headband of rosebuds.

'You look gorgeous!' Jasmine breathed in awe. But then she didn't realise how she looked herself. Rachel just stared back in amazement and said, 'So do you!'

She called her gran. 'Gran, come and see us!'

'Lovely, dear,' said her gran, but she didn't smile. In fact as she looked at the two of them together standing side by side holding hands – black hand in white hand – she frowned.

The next day, Rachel wasn't down at the playing fields as arranged. Jasmine bounced up and down on the end of the seesaw waiting and waiting, but Rachel didn't come. Finally, Jasmine went round to Rachel's house and knocked on the door. It was grandmother again, who answered.

'Rachel's out,' she informed her curtly, and slammed the door.

Jasmine went home and Lena said, 'You're back quickly. Couldn't Rachel play today?'

'Nope,' snapped Jasmine abruptly.

'What's up, love?' asked Lena putting a

loving arm around her.

'Nothing,' muttered Jasmine, stiffening and pulling away. Then she rushed up to her room and didn't even look at Bramble who stood nearby with his tail wagging expectantly.

The next day, Jasmine waited as usual for Rachel to come down to play at the swings. She waited and waited, but when Rachel didn't come, she wandered along on her own. Rachel was there already chatting in a group with Melanie and Tracey.

Jasmine waved and smiled, but Rachel only gave a half-wave back, then bent her head into the group and took no more notice of her.

Jasmine sat dejectedly on the end of the seesaw. Rachel didn't come and join her. Some of the other children began to whisper and snigger among themselves. Some glanced over their shoulders at her and then bent their heads together as if plotting something.

Suddenly Rachel got up and walked away. Jasmine ran over to her, and for a while they walked towards the gates in silence. Then Jasmine said, in a small, uneasy voice, 'What's up, Rachel? Aren't we friends no more?'

'Yes, of course we are . . . I mean . . .' Rachel blushed bright red. 'It's just . . .'

'Why aren't you talking to me? Why aren't you playing with me? I waited for you and you didn't come,' cried Jasmine in a rush of accusations. 'What's wrong?'

116

'Nothing,' murmured Rachel, but she sighed deeply.

'Would you like to come round to my house?' suggested Jasmine. 'We could make *pappadums.*'

'I can't,' said Rachel. 'It's my gran, you see . . . when Mum gets back, perhaps . . .' Her voice trailed away with embarrassment.

'Shall I call for you tomorrow, then?' asked Jasmine. 'You could tell me about the baby, you being an aunt and all that.'

'No. You'd better not.' Then Rachel turned and ran off home.

When Jasmine got home she was crying.

'Why, darling, whatever's the matter?' asked Lena rushing over to her. This time, she didn't touch her, but just stood close like a great rock for Jasmine to hang on to if she chose to. 'What is it, Jasmine?' she asked.

'It's nothing,' snorted Jasmine.

'Of course it's not nothing, come on, tell me.'

'Nobody loves me,' stammered Jasmine. 'No one wants to play with me. I want to go back to Aunty Sheila's.'

'Oh no, Jasmine!' cried Lena with alarm. 'But that's not true. Lots of people love you. Bob and I, we love you so much we want you to be our daughter. Bramble loves you. Look at him!' Bramble had come and leaned against Jasmine's knees, trying to lick her salty tears as they fell from her eyes. 'And then there's

117

Rachel. She loves you. She's your best friend!'
urged Lena.

'No, she doesn't. No, she isn't. She's not my
friend any more,' gulped Jasmine, and sobbed
even louder.

'Saints alive! Of course she is. Why you two
have been like Siamese twins all summer long.
The whole neighbourhood knows it.'

'Well, she isn't now,' repeated Jasmine. 'She
won't call for me; she won't wait for me, and
she won't play with me on the swings. She
says I shouldn't call for her tomorrow neither.
She just doesn't like me any more.'

Lena shook her head in disbelief. 'She can't
stop liking you, just like that. Maybe she just
wasn't feeling herself. It can happen to anyone.
You see. Tomorrow will be just fine.'

But tomorrow wasn't just fine. The same
thing happened. Jasmine went down to the
swings alone and came back alone. Lena was
looking out of the window and saw her
coming. 'Didn't Rachel play with you today?'
she asked anxiously.

'Nope,' answered Jasmine in a dull voice. 'I
told you. She doesn't like me any more.'

'Something must have happened,' said
Lena. 'You must have quarrelled or done
something.'

'Nope,' said Jasmine, sullen. 'Nothing.'
Then she said, 'I wish I was white,' and rushed
away upstairs.

When Bob came home that night, Lena told him everything. Bob said, 'Have you tried speaking to Rachel's mum? You and she were quite friendly, weren't you? Even from before Jasmine came along.'

'Yes . . . I suppose I should . . .' murmured Lena. 'Though I don't like interfering with kids' affairs. I suppose it's their business if they don't want to be friends. Still . . . this is important. I'll try.' She went to the phone.

Of course, Rachel's mum wasn't there. Her grandmother answered, at first in a warm polite voice. But when she knew who was calling, she became cold as ice and told her that Rachel's mother was away till Thursday.

'Oh,' said Lena. 'Then I'll wait till then to speak to her,' and hung up looking flushed and furious.

'What's up, love?' asked Bob anxiously. 'Don't tell me you and she have fallen out too?'

'Nope, she's not there. Barbara's gone away. Back Thursday . . . it's that . . . it's her . . . mum . . . I wonder.'

'Wonder what?' asked Bob, mystified.

'I think it's all because of Rachel's grandmother. She doesn't like black people.'

When Bob tucked Jasmine up in bed that night, he whispered, 'Jasmine, darling. You just listen to me. We live in a cruel old world. Children are cruel and grown-ups too. They'll always find things to pick on. If you're fat or wear glasses or . . . do you know what? My ears used to stick out when I was a kid. Hated it. All my mates called me "Big Ears" and I was so miserable, I wanted to have an operation. Of course I grew my hair long so that it covered my ears, but one thing you can't do is hide the colour of your skin. Some people don't like you just because you're black. Isn't that daft? If you were mean, nasty, cheating, greedy, those would be good reasons to hate you. But just to hate because of your colour . . . that's really cruel. So you have to be brave and grow a tough skin over your black skin so as not to get hurt. But you know what? I'm sure that Rachel loves you. I'm not stupid. I've seen the way you play together. I think things will be O.K. in a day or two.'

'When her mum gets back?' asked Jasmine.

'Maybe,' said Bob.

But that night, Jasmine crept downstairs and slept in the dog basket, and once more, Bramble moved out and slept on the rug in front of the fireplace.

Lena couldn't help crying. Everything was back to square one. Jasmine was once more the cold, silent child they had first met in the children's home. She slumped in front of the television set, not smiling, not looking at them and refusing to go out.

'It's not going to work, is it!' wept Lena. 'We're not the right people for her.'

'We've got to be patient,' murmured Bob, comfortingly. But inside, he too felt in despair as he set out for work.

Lena tried to persuade Jasmine to come shopping with her, but Jasmine rudely turned her head away and muttered, 'Go by yourself.'

'I don't like leaving you alone,' said Lena, 'so I'll leave Bramble with you for company.' Then taking her shopping basket, she left the house with a heavy heart.

For a long while Jasmine didn't move. She sat on the settee in a huddle, her arms clasped around her knees and her head down. Bramble came and stood nearby wagging his tail and making little noises in his throat to catch her attention. But at first Jasmine wouldn't even look at him. He came closer and licked her clenched fingers. She softened slightly and scratched him under his chin with just one finger. He came closer and leant heavily against her knees and gave a little whine. It was the whine he made when he wanted to go out.

'Oh, Bramble!' cried Jasmine, flinging her arms around his neck. 'Do you want to be my friend? Because nobody else does.' Then she jumped up and said, 'O.K. If you want to go out, I'll take you. Why shouldn't I? We're friends, aren't we?'

She ran to the kitchen where Bramble's lead hung from a hook. She took it down. The jangle and clang of the chain made Bramble very excited. He jumped and twisted and wagged his tail furiously. He nearly knocked Jasmine over in his excitement. 'Keep still, silly boy!' she begged him, as she tried to get the lead over his head. Then at last she did it. 'I'll show them that I can take you to the park. You'll listen to me, won't you!'

She opened the door and was barely able to close it behind her as Bramble dragged her down the path on to the pavement.

It would have been hard to tell whether Jasmine was taking Bramble for a walk or Bramble was taking Jasmine. He tugged so hard, she almost flew along towards the park. As she came through the park gates, she saw lots of children clustered round the swings. Rachel was there and Melanie and Tracey, and there was Rachel's dog, Polly, tied up as usual to one of the poles. Jasmine forgot all her troubles and began racing across the grass with Bramble bounding and barking with joy at her side.

'Hi, Rachel! Hi, Melanie, Tracey! Look! I've brought Bramble down to the swings too. He knows me now!' and she tied him up alongside Polly.

'Hi, Jasmine!' said Rachel, but she went red and seemed embarrassed as all the other children turned and stared.

Jasmine went to the seesaw. She didn't sit

down at one end, this time, but stood astride the middle, her feet balanced on either side so that she could tip the seesaw this way and that.

Once again the children began to whisper and snigger among themselves. They looked across at her and pulled faces. Then a big boy called out, 'Hey, what's that smell?'

Another cried, 'It's coming from the seesaw.'

'Ugh!' sneered another voice. 'Look at that! Where did that come from?'

The children turned towards her now and began to advance menacingly. They chanted: 'Look at her funny hair! Look at her squidgey nose! Look at her silly face. We don't like people like you. Go away! Go away!' They jumped around her, pulling faces.

Jasmine turned into a statue on the seesaw. She wanted to run away, but her body wouldn't move. The voices were ugly, the faces full of cruelty.

Jasmine saw Rachel. She was watching the scene from the other side of the playground. She began to move towards the chanting children. Her face had no expression. 'Was she . . .? Would she . . .? Surely she wouldn't join in? Would she?' Jasmine watched her coming nearer and nearer. She stopped. Their eyes met. Rachel's face went red. Jasmine bowed her head and began to mutter to herself.

'What you say is what you are. What you say

is what you are.' She said it louder and louder until she was shouting it.

Rachel's face was red, but it was red with anger. She got angrier and angrier. She pushed through the children, even though they were bigger than her. She rushed up to Jasmine and was about to take her hand, when someone undid Bramble and shooed him away.

With a scream of horror, Jasmine sprang from the seesaw and went chasing after him. Behind her she could hear the voices shouting after her. 'Go away, go away! Go back where you came from!'

Jasmine was running. Suddenly it seemed as if the whole world was spinning. The earth beneath her feet seemed to rotate taking her through day and night, night and day in rapid succession, while above her head, the clouds whirled by and sun and moon came and went like tossing boats.

The voices of the children rose on the wind and screamed with the gulls and crows and all the time her own voice beat like a drum, 'What you say is what you are . . . What you say is what you are.'

Bramble had vanished. Jasmine searched the park from end to end. She went down to the little stream, she called and called and whistled and shouted his name, but he didn't appear. How could she go back without him? She wandered back towards the swings. The children had gone now. As the sun sank slowly, she could see the chains hanging loosely and abandoned and the seesaw an empty slant against the sky. She wandered slowly over and sat down on one end. In the distance she could see the park keeper. Soon he would come and shoo her out of the park before locking up.

She got up and began to walk towards the back gates. She wouldn't go home. She'd run away. No one would love her now. Now that Bramble was lost, Lena and Bob wouldn't love her either.

The park keeper waved his stick at her. 'Oi! You can't go out that way! I've locked up. You'll have to go out the front.'

As she turned towards the front gates, she suddenly saw a small speck of a figure racing across the grass towards her with ponytail flying and a dog bounding along at her side. It was Rachel, only the dog . . . the dog wasn't Polly . . . it was . . . Bramble!

Jasmine shouted for joy. 'Bramble, Bramble! Here, boy!' Rachel let go of the lead and the dog came hurtling over to Jasmine and nearly knocked her to the ground with excitement.

Rachel ran up panting hard, her eyes glowing with satisfaction.

'Oh thank you, thank you!' cried Jasmine. 'Where did you find him?'

'He went home. I knew he would,' said

Rachel proudly.

Waiting over at the gates were Bob and Lena. When Jasmine saw them, she gave Rachel the lead and began running towards them as fast as she could. Thrusting an arm into each of theirs she looked up with a glowing face. 'Can Rachel come to tea?' she asked.

Bob and Lena nodded. They knew everything was going to be all right. As Rachel came up to them, Jasmine said, 'You can come over to my house if you like, and . . .' She looked up at Lena. 'Will you make *pappadums* for us?'

'Of course,' laughed Lena.

'And shall we play dressing up?' asked Rachel.

'Yes, let's!' cried Jasmine happily.

As they walked home Jasmine said, 'When we go to the big school, shall you and me sit together?'

That night Bob and Lena put Jasmine to bed in her own bed in her own room. They wondered where they would find her the next morning. When the morning came, they went downstairs. They looked under the kitchen table and the dining-room table, behind the settee and in the coat cupboard. Bramble was in his basket and thumped his tail sleepily as though to say, 'She didn't sleep here last night.'

Then Bob and Lena looked at each other. Could it be? At last? They went back upstairs and quietly tiptoed into Jasmine's bedroom. There was a hump under the bedclothes and a black curly head on the pillow. At last they knew. Jasmine was here to stay.

When Jasmine and Rachel went up to the comprehensive, they went into the same class. They sat side by side in every lesson. They went round together, ate school dinners together and went home together. In fact no one ever saw Jasmine without Rachel or Rachel without Jasmine. But one thing did change. Now when anyone asked Jasmine what her name was, she replied, 'My name is Jasmine Jacobs,' and no one quite understood why she said it with such a big smile.

A Selected List of Fiction from Mammoth

While every effort is made to keep prices low, it is sometimes necessary to increase prices at short notice. Mammoth Books reserves the right to show new retail prices on covers which may differ from those previously advertised in the text or elsewhere.

The prices shown below were correct at the time of going to press.

☐	7497 0366 0	**Dilly the Dinosaur**	Tony Bradman £1.99
☐	7497 0021 1	**Dilly and the Tiger**	Tony Bradman £1.99
☐	7497 0137 4	**Flat Stanley**	Jeff Brown £1.99
☐	7497 0048 3	**Friends and Brothers**	Dick King-Smith £1.99
☐	7497 0054 8	**My Naughty Little Sister**	Dorothy Edwards £1.99
☐	416 86550 X	**Cat Who Wanted to go Home**	Jill Tomlinson £1.99
☐	7497 0166 8	**The Witch's Big Toe**	Ralph Wright £1.99
☐	7497 0218 4	**Lucy Jane at the Ballet**	Susan Hampshire £2.25
☐	416 03212 5	**I Don't Want To!**	Bel Mooney £1.99
☐	7497 0030 0	**I Can't Find It!**	Bel Mooney £1.99
☐	7497 0032 7	**The Bear Who Stood on His Head**	W. J. Corbett £1.99
☐	416 10362 6	**Owl and Billy**	Martin Waddell £1.75
☐	416 13822 5	**It's Abigail Again**	Moira Miller £1.75
☐	7497 0031 9	**King Tubbitum and the Little Cook**	Margaret Ryan £1.99
☐	7497 0041 6	**The Quiet Pirate**	Andrew Matthews £1.99
☐	7497 0064 5	**Grump and the Hairy Mammoth**	Derek Sampson £1.99

All these books are available at your bookshop or newsagent, or can be ordered direct from the publisher. Just tick the titles you want and fill in the form below.

Mandarin Paperbacks, Cash Sales Department, PO Box 11, Falmouth, Cornwall TR10 9EN.

Please send cheque or postal order, no currency, for purchase price quoted and allow the following for postage and packing:

UK   80p for the first book, 20p for each additional book ordered to a maximum charge of £2.00.

BFPO   80p for the first book, 20p for each additional book.

Overseas   £1.50 for the first book, £1.00 for the second and 30p for each additional book including Eire thereafter.

NAME (Block letters) ....

ADDRESS ....

....

....